"You're still here."

Gabe—all rumpled six foot two of him—turned toward Evangeline and frowned. "I told you I wasn't leaving you."

They were just words. She knew that. Throwaways. Meaningless. Chosen with care and delivered with skill, just like everything Gabriel Fontenot did. Memory flashed before she could stop it: Gabe in his office and the look in his eyes, the feel of his mouth and the taste of his kiss, the desperation and the needs and the—

Blocking the image, she destroyed it, but his words kept winding through her, dangerously close to the place she could not allow him to touch.

"I know this is the last place you want to be," she said.

"That's where you're wrong, *catin*," he murmured, stalking closer. Too close. "I can't think of *anywhere* else I'd rather be."

Dear Reader,

People often ask me where my characters come from. It's a great question—but hard to answer! The characters are just…there. They live in my heart, as real to me as flesh-and-blood friends. Some allow me to have a tidy business relationship with them. They move in, I tell their story, then we're done.

Gabriel Fontenot is not such a character. Gabe showed up as a secondary character, a laid-back attorney with a smooth smile and a fondness for poker. Easy enough. Laid-back. Sexy. Confident. Check, check, check.

But Gabe's life imploded, and letters from readers flooded my mailbox, demanding that I fix him. That I give Gabe his own story—the happily ever after he deserved. Wow, when he and I got busy, I realized my easygoing, sexy lawyer had become a complex man. He and I wrestled a lot, and sometimes I wanted to smack him. You might, too. But in the end, his heart of gold led the way, and I cried when he found his way out of the darkness. I hope you will, too.

Happy reading,

Jenna Mills

Jenna Mills

A LITTLE BIT
GUILTY

Romantic
SUSPENSE

SILHOUETTE BOOKS

ISBN-13: 978-0-373-27538-0
ISBN-10:   0-373-27538-2

A LITTLE BIT GUILTY

Copyright © 2007 by Jennifer Miller

Books by Jenna Mills

Silhouette Romantic Suspense

Smoke and Mirrors #1146
When Night Falls #1170
The Cop Next Door #1181
A Kiss in the Dark #1199
The Perfect Target #1212
Crossfire #1275
Shock Waves #1287
A Cry in the Dark #1299
*The Perfect Stranger #1461
*A Little Bit Guilty #1468

*Midnight Secrets

JENNA MILLS

Stories set in the South come naturally to bestselling author Jenna Mills. Born and raised in Louisiana, she cut her teeth early on the myths and legends of the Old South—and couldn't get enough of old plantation ruins! She started creating stories of her own as soon as she could talk, and when she mastered pen and paper, those stories found their way into notebooks. Now she's still telling stories...still captivated by mystery—and romance.

A member of Romance Writers of America, Dallas Area Romance Authors and North Louisiana Storytellers, Jenna has earned critical acclaim for her stories of deep emotion, steamy romance and page-turning suspense. When not writing, Jenna spends her time with her young daughter and her husband, as well as a house full of cats, dogs and plants. You can visit Jenna at her Web site, www.jennamills.com, or drop her a note at P.O. Box 768, Coppell, TX 75019.

This one's for Simon, the most amazing companion ever. This was our last book together, and whenever I think of Gabe's story, I'll think of all the sunny afternoons you stretched out alongside my computer and purred while I wrote. I miss you, big guy; thanks for four beautiful years. I wish there could have been more, but love never dies.

And as always, for my husband and my daughter— for the smiles, the patience, the inspiration and, most of all, the love.

Chapter 1

Assistant District Attorney Gabriel Fontenot did his best work in the dark.

Standing silently in an old warehouse that had been submerged during hurricane Katrina, he refused to let himself move, barely let himself breathe. Much of New Orleans had recovered. Homes were being rebuilt. Stores had restocked their shelves. Music again pulsed through the city, a touch of Hispanic added to the blues. Even tourists once more swarmed the French Quarter.

The city who charmed by day and seduced by night was on her way back.

But here on the fringes, squalor remained.

The night bled in, thick and suffocating despite the early-March breeze swirling outside. Away from the city, moonlight seeped in through the windows, but the smear of mud and grime revealed little more than shapes and shadows.

A metal wall guarded Gabe's back, stacks of empty crates took care of the rest. No one would find him unless he wanted them to. But Gabe did not allow himself to relax. Either a man learned from his mistakes, or he lost.

Gabe had no intention of losing.

The emaciated dogs had run off, leaving silence to throb through the warehouse, broken only by the occasional horn of a tugboat. There was no trace of the waitress who'd insisted they meet privately. Fear had flared in her eyes when she'd realized who he was and what he wanted. She'd paled, panicked.

And inside, for the first time in weeks, Gabe had smiled.

She knew something. A name, a place, any little detail that could link the senseless murder of a fellow waitress to the high-profile restaurateur who'd written both their paychecks. That was all Gabe wanted. A scrap, a crumb.

He could take it from there.

Young and scared, she'd refused to speak to him in the French Quarter restaurant where she continued to wait tables despite the murder of her coworker. Unwilling to so much as take his drink order, she'd gone on a sudden break—but not before slipping him a cocktail napkin with detailed instructions about where she *would* talk to him.

Restless, Gabe moved away from the crates. His watch showed that almost thirty minutes had passed. If the waitress was going to show, she would have done so by now.

And if she was going to approach him, she wouldn't stop moving every time he did.

Through the darkness he heard the muffled movement behind him. And when he stopped, it stopped. And, damn it, he was so freaking tired of running in circles and chasing phantoms. Him. Gabriel Fontenot. The man who could bluff an opponent into folding, even when Gabe had nothing but a handful of trash.

It had been a long time since he'd held anything else.

Jaw clenched, he retraced his steps, confident the maze of crates would conceal him until it was too late for his pursuer to realize that the hunter had become the hunted.

He was a lawyer by training, a man of tailored suits, leather briefcases and expensive loafers. It was his cousin who was the cop. But Cain had taught him well.

Against the trickle of moonlight, the silhouette stood without moving. Except for the breathing. Gabe heard each rasp, felt them ricochet through his body. Fear had a taste and feel unto itself and, despite the darkness, he knew his target realized the tables had turned. Tall, he noted. Far too tall to be the petite waitress he'd met earlier that evening.

Quietly he lunged—and the shadow bolted.

Gabe gave chase, grabbing the high-powered flashlight from his pocket and flicking it on. The shadow boxer-danced around a shopping cart and sent it careening toward Gabe. Shoving against it, he sent it crashing to its side as he veered around an old piano just as the figure darted behind more crates. Gabe charged, sending the stack crashing down.

The distorted grunt told him they'd found their target.

Rounding the pile, he saw the man scrambling to his

feet. "Freeze," he called. "I have a gun." He didn't, but the punk didn't know that.

The beam of Gabe's flashlight caught the man who'd been following him, revealing dark jeans and a bulky field jacket with a fleur-de-lis across the back, a baseball cap pulled low.

"Raise your hands and turn around," Gabe instructed. "Nice and slow."

From somewhere in the warehouse, the dogs were barking, but Gabe ignored them and focused on his man. Two weeks before, the intruder trying to break into his house had gotten away. He had no intention of history repeating itself.

"Now," he said, directing his light to the man's hands, where he saw gloves, but no gun, "don't make me ask again."

The man didn't. He called Gabe's bluff and ran.

On a low roar Gabe lunged after him, keeping the fleur-de-lis locked in the beam of his flashlight. The front door was less than ten feet away. If the idiot got outside—

With a burst of speed Gabe launched himself like a veteran linebacker driving a rookie receiver into the turf.

The impact of body against body jolted through him. He felt more than heard the other man's breath leave his body as they slammed into the concrete. But he didn't relax, didn't pull back, instead used his weight to pin the fool to the ground. "You have exactly five seconds to start talking."

The body beneath his stilled.

"Three seconds," Gabe gritted out, pressing his hands against shoulders that felt surprisingly thin. That's when he noticed the hair. Dislodged during the struggle, the baseball cap fell to the side, revealing a swingy fall of brown hair.

Soft. Silky.

"What the he—" he started, but the body beneath his twisted, and a pair of tilted gray eyes met his.

"Gabe."

The sound of her voice, hoarser than usual, slammed into him. Then came the burn. It started low and sliced fast, obliterating everything but the sight of her sprawled beneath him. Her skin was flushed, her mouth slightly open, just as it had been—

He blocked the memory, focused only on her eyes, wide and dark and drenched with a wildness that fired his blood—and resurrected every fragmented image he'd tried to destroy. Every touch. Every kiss. Every lie.

Every betrayal.

"Well, well, well," he drawled, because for the first time in months, he no longer held a hand of junk. He held *her.* "If it's not lady justice in the flesh."

The district attorney's little darling. The media's champion. The common man's avenging angel. Evangeline Rousseau—the woman who'd reeled him in with the finesse of a pro, then hung him out to dry.

"You just can't stay away from me, can you, *catin?*" The slow smile was the first to reach his mouth in a damn long time. "Even when you should."

No.

The word scraped through her, but Evangeline refused to give it voice, just as she refused to beg or apologize. Not to this man. He would see only what he wanted to see. Believe only what he wanted to believe.

Especially when it came to her.

Against the throb of pain at her temple she narrowed her eyes and tried to reconcile her last sight of him— clean-shaven in a devastatingly well-cut tuxedo—with the man who held her pinned to the concrete. The attorney with a taste for Armani wore a knit cap over his dark hair, with whiskers obscuring his jaw and violence glittering in his eyes.

It was a far cry from the way he'd looked at her once, when he'd found a way to touch her without lifting a hand.

The vertigo wobbled closer, no matter how hard she tried to ignore the cold soaking into her stomach and thighs. Once his touch had been one of friendship and warmth. Then heat. Now his hands curled around her upper arms, while his thighs sandwiched her lower back.

"This is a good look for you," he said, and if she'd had any doubt about his state of mind, his deceptively quiet voice took care of that. It was the attorney's voice, the signature gentle lull he used during opening statements to bond with the jury. Just before he went for the jugular. "If Judge Guidry had gotten a look at you like this, you might not have lost—"

And she wasn't going to let him do it. Wasn't going to let him attack, wasn't going to let him pretend that he was the victim.

"Get off me—" She twisted against him…but the warehouse twisted with her, started to spin. "Th-this isn't…what you think," she managed, but the vertigo tilted harder.

Not much light broke the shadows, only that from the beam of his flashlight. But it was enough to reveal the slow smile curving his lips. "Oh, but I think it is."

Maybe she should have been afraid. Most women would have been. He'd caught her red-handed—again. They were alone, and he'd been pushed too far. He knew too much, would try to cram pieces together until they fit, even if they had nothing to do with each other.

"We're finally alone," he drawled, "just like you wanted from the start. So tell me. What happens now?"

The quickening was as violent as it was automatic. She couldn't remember the last day she'd awakened without thinking—

But that wasn't true. She could remember. It had been summer.

She'd been eighteen years old.

"You have no idea what I wanted," she said—she'd made very, very sure of that. But the words came out thicker than she wanted. The pain came next, stabbing with sharp streaks of blue and white. "I—I…can't breathe," she managed.

"Maybe you should have thought of that before you followed me into a dark warehouse," he said, and though it was Gabe who spoke, it was not the man she'd met four months before who she heard. "No telling what could happen…who you might run into." Some said that man no longer existed—too much whiskey, too many pills.

"Maybe even someone who doesn't know when to stop," he added quietly and, for the first time, she questioned the wisdom of following him into the shadows.

Shifting, he raised up on his knees and eased his weight from her body.

She seized the opportunity and tried to push from beneath him, realized her mistake too late.

Within seconds she was flat on her back, and he still straddled her body.

"Tell me something, *catin*. Was this part of your plan, too? Getting me on top of you?"

The French word for doll scraped. She wanted to shove against him, to push him off her body and—

That was just it. There was no *and*. She couldn't go back and change what had already happened. She couldn't erase the fact that he'd found her here, in this warehouse. Following him.

She could only pick up the pieces and move forward, the way she'd been doing since the night he'd frozen her out of his life three months before.

"What's wrong? Last time wasn't enough for you?" It was the attorney's voice again, pressing, driving for a confession. "My trust…my respect…*my job*—you still want more?" Bracing his hands against the concrete, he leaned closer. "Who sent you here?" His voice was razor soft. "Whose puppet are you *this* time?"

The warehouse started to spin. Slowly at first. Faster. "Did it ever occur to you," she whispered, "that I'm here to help?"

His eyes gleamed. "And just how are you going to do that?"

"I—I got a phone call." She chose her words carefully, even as they tried to scatter. "A little over an hour ago. From an informant."

Through the shadows, Gabe's expression gave away nothing.

"They said they had information for me. About—" the victim's named slipped away "—the murdered girl—and Marcel Lambert."

"Male or female?"

"Female." She swallowed against the cottony dryness. "They gave me this address… Said I'd find something interesting."

His smile was pure, classic Gabriel Fontenot on the hunt. "So you followed me."

Just as she'd been doing for weeks. After the discovery that Gabe's fiancée had been selling critical information about pending cases to the highest bidder, he'd been placed on leave. He was damaged goods, a liability. By no means was he supposed to be anywhere near the delicate case they were building against Marcel Lambert—it wasn't every day one of New Orleans's finest stood accused of murdering a prostitute. But Gabe had been poking around, anyway, asking questions, sifting through the debris of Darci Falgoust's shattered life.

And Evangeline wanted to know why—and what he'd found.

"Not at first." She hedged as the sound of something falling echoed through the warehouse. She glanced toward the old piano, wished she hadn't. Everything shifted with her, spun.

"I…waited." Through sheer grit she kept her voice steady. "I thought I'd…" The words rolled away.

She searched for them, tried to yank them back. Didn't understand why her voice slurred. "Thought I'd see what was going on when you came out." For twenty-three minutes she'd stood with her back to the warehouse, watching. Or, at least, she thought it had been twenty-three minutes. But like curtains in the breeze, her memory floated in and out of focus. "But you never came out."

Eyes flat, he eased away and crossed his arms over his chest. "So you came in after me."

"Yes." She blinked hard, brought the smear of red against his knuckles into focus. "You should do something about that."

He didn't move. "Why did you run from me?"

"It was dark—I didn't know it was you." To make her point, she flicked her eyes toward the stocking cap that made him look more like a meth addict than the respected attorney he'd once been. "I—I've never seen you like this."

But she'd heard the rumors….

"Nice story." His tone was mild, as it always was when a defendant wrapped up his alibi. "Now let me tell you what I see." He hesitated, the way he so often did in the courtroom, leaving only the scream of crickets to fill the silence. "It's late. I've got a meeting. But instead of my informant I find you sneaking around—my so-called colleague, who fed me dirty information less than three months ago."

He made it sound so reprehensible, when in reality, there'd been every reason to believe he was the one compromising case after case.

"It was an Internal Affairs investigation, Gabe." One that ultimately had led them to his lover—and almost cost Gabe his life. But when the smoke cleared, it was Val who'd lain dead. "That hardly makes me guilty of some great heinous crime."

The cobalt of his eyes glowed. "What's the payoff?" He kept on with the bulldog focus that had always defined him. "You think you can manipulate me again? You think proving I'm not following the rules gives you some kind of leverage over me?"

The faint scent of whiskey disturbed in ways she refused to analyze. "You've been drinking…" She sidestepped his questions.

"I've been doing a lot of things, sweetness—you want names and dates and places? Would that help you, Evang—" His eyes warmed, even as they chilled. "Or maybe I should just call you *Eve.*"

The warehouse took a hard tilt to the left.

"Sorry, *catin,*" he drawled again, this time with another slow smile. "But I'm not interested in another apple."

Ten seconds. That was the difference between being caught and being free. If she hadn't slammed into the edge of a big-screen TV, Gabe would never have caught her.

"Black-and-white." She realized. "That's all you see, isn't it?" All he'd ever seen. "You really want to sit here and tell me you wouldn't have done the same thing?"

His eyes met hers. "Make someone trust me so I can hang them out to dry? Hate to break it to you, *catin,* but you must not have done your homework, after all."

Oh, but she had. "What do you want from me?" She hated the way her heart kept banging against her ribs. "For me to tell you I'm sorry? I've—" Again the words slipped away. And again she reached for them. "I've already done that." On more than one occasion. "If I recall, it didn't do much good."

His finger came to rest against her cheekbone. "You sure you want to know what I want?"

Maybe it was the way he asked the question. Or maybe it was the way he looked at her, touched her, the way he still straddled her. But all those reasons she had to mistrust this man blurred. *"Yes."*

His eyes were flat, giving neither mercy nor reprieve nor warning. She'd played poker with him once— without one full house, one four-of-a-kind, he'd walked away with five grand.

"How about the truth," he said. "Once and for all. How far would you have taken your little game? I think about that sometimes… How far you would have gone? You let me touch you…kiss you. You let me believe—"

She didn't want to think about what he'd been about to say. What he'd been through in the months since his world had imploded.

"How much more were you willing to lay on the line?" he asked after a long silence. "What would have happened if I hadn't pulled back?"

She would have pulled back. She. Would. Have.

"What do you want me to say?" she asked. "That I would have gone to bed with you? Is that what you—"

Movement to the right killed her words. She glanced over, wished she hadn't. Everything shifted.

Blinking, she'd grabbed Gabe's thigh before she remembered there was nothing else to grab. Then she saw the dogs. Two of them watching from beside a pile of crates. "R-Rebel?"

Against her cheek, Gabe's hand stilled. "Rebel?" he repeated, twisting toward the crates. "What the hell—"

The emaciated yellow Lab slunk toward the old piano, never taking his eyes off her. "My…dog." He watched her, his ribs bowing out with each pant. "I—I haven't seen him in…" Seven years. Since he'd crossed the rainbow bridge after sixteen years of companionship. Alarmed, because Rebel was there and wouldn't stop staring at her through those haunted chocolate eyes, she closed her own and sucked in a shaky breath.

"Evangeline."

The edge to Gabe's voice penetrated the fog; quieter, not the antagonistic growl of the vigilante who'd tackled her, but…Gabe's voice. *Gabe.* The seemingly laid-back

Southern attorney she'd first been introduced to over a pot of burned coffee a few months before. "Open your eyes."

She didn't want to. She didn't want the voice to go away. She didn't want to see the hard lines of a mouth that had once been dangerously soft. She wanted to stay in this alternate reality where she could let herself believe that if she did open her eyes, it wouldn't be contempt blazing back at her.

And Rebel wouldn't be watching from a few feet away.

"Jesus," Gabe said. "You're hurt."

She opened her eyes and found them kneeling beside her, both of them, Gabe and Rebel. Gabe's hand, she would have sworn, shook as it reached for her. But because that made no sense, she blinked. And this time Rebel vanished.

"What day is this?" Gabe's voice was thicker now, strained, like a witness forced to confront a brutal detail they'd tried to scrub from their memory.

"Mon—" The flash of white stopped her. "Tuesday." It had to be. She'd watched her favorite reality show the night before, and it aired on Mondays.

"What month?"

This time she thought before speaking. "March." Darci had been killed in January, Marcel Lambert arrested in late February.

Gabe took her hand and eased her toward him, holding on until she sat upright. "Who am I?"

She looked down at their palms pressed together, the trickle of blood seeping from between his fingers to hers. Then she looked up. Around them only the residue of silence remained. The dog was gone. The crickets were quiet.

The urge to lift her hand to his face was strong. She wanted to feel the roughness against her fingertips. The soft prickle of his whiskers. She wanted to rub her thumb along the mouth that had once slanted so hungrily against hers, to convince herself that the moment was real. That the way he looked at her was real. That the contempt was the illusion.

"You're Gabe," she said, and somewhere deep inside, a window shattered. She knew better than to want…than to reach…but couldn't make herself stop. "You're here."

Shadows played against him, darkening his eyes. For a moment he said nothing, just looked down at her as though he'd never seen her before. Then, slowly, he pulled his hand from hers and brought it to her temple. There she felt two fingers skim lightly.

And when he pulled back, she saw blood.

His, she told herself. Gabe's. It was his hand that was bleeding. Then he folded down several fingers.

She blinked. And she swallowed. And everything shifted. Faster, the light and the dark and the shadows, the crates and the dogs—and a piano? But there were four dogs now. Four skinny yellow Labs. And no matter how hard she tried to lock on to Gabe's fingers, she saw five, even though she knew he held two against his palm.

And finally she realized what was going on.

"Three," she guessed, not wanting him to know that, when he'd tackled her, her head had bounced against the concrete. That's why her thoughts kept scattering, why she thought she saw concern glimmering in his eyes.

That was why she had to get away from him before she said or did something that could not be taken back.

"Sweet good God," he muttered, moving so fast her own heart started to race. "Two," he all but growled as he reached for her and stood. In some faraway corner of her mind she knew she should struggle, find some way to twist away from him. She didn't want him to touch her. She didn't want his help. She knew better than to trust or believe or…

Want. God help her, she knew better than to want.

But the protests disintegrated before she could grab on to them, and then there was only Gabe, kicking open the door and carrying her into the cool March night.

Later, she promised herself. Later. After her head quit throbbing, after the world quit spinning, then she would think. Then she would plan, find some way to undo the damage and make sure Gabriel Fontenot paid for the life he'd taken.

Later…

After she closed her eyes.

After she regathered.

After being in his arms quit feeling so horribly right.

Chapter 2

He watched her sleep.

Beneath a patchwork quilt, she lay on her side, her knees bent and her arms curved toward her face, dark hair spilling against the pillow. He'd closed the blinds, but moonlight slipped through the slats and fell against her face. Her eyes and mouth were relaxed, the bandage at her temple barely visible.

By her side, a big Siamese cat tracked Gabe's every move. Simon, she'd called him when he'd sharpened his already-sharp claws against the side of her sofa.

Walk away, Gabe told himself. Not because of the commando cat, but because he didn't want to see her this way, soft and vulnerable and...hurt. He needed to see her as she'd been before, when she'd touched him and kissed him, while the whole time she'd been methodically hanging him out to dry.

Now…Christ. *Now.* He didn't want to be here, in her loft, in her bedroom that smelled of powder and vanilla, with half-burned candles on the dresser and fuzzy slippers on the floor. He wanted to be back at the warehouse, looking for the waitress. The questions just kept mounting—for all he knew she'd never intended to talk…she was on someone's payroll…the whole thing had been a setup. And Evangeline had walked straight into the cross fire.

Or maybe she'd been the one firing.

A concussion, the doctor at the clinic had said. Minor, but serious enough that Evangeline shouldn't be left alone. She needed to be watched, monitored.

But, sweet mercy, the doctor hadn't meant every second of every minute of every hour.

Four months had passed since Evangeline had strolled into the D.A.'s office with a grace and confidence that had damn near knocked him flat, like the girl-next-door all grown-up and dressed in a killer suit. She'd smiled and offered first her hand, then her friendship. Then so much more.

He'd never seen the knife coming, not until she'd embedded it in his back.

The quick stab at his temple made him wince. He braced himself and closed his eyes, knew the onslaught that awaited. For a time, the headaches had been a daily occurrence. Tension, his doctor maintained. Stress. When his life settled back into normalcy, they would go away. It sounded pretty damn simplistic, but the thought of being headache free—*of being pill free*—had seduced. So he'd tried.

But then the young French Quarter waitress had been

found murdered; her employer, Marcel Lambert, implicated. It seemed he'd been paying her for more than waiting tables, and with his arrest, Gabe's headaches had just…stopped. Maybe crime and punishment weren't normalcy for the average person, but that had changed for Gabe one rainy night almost a quarter of a century before.

There could be no normalcy for him, not until Marcel Lambert paid for his sins.

Opening his eyes, Gabe looked at Evangeline lying between the soft floral sheets. *Sleeping.* She'd changed into an oversized T-shirt and crawled into bed, closed her eyes and gone to sleep. With him right there, in her loft. *Him.* The man everyone said was spinning out of control. She was a smart woman. She knew better than to lower her guard like that, to close her eyes and let go, to trust…him.

The fact that she did made his temple throb harder.

The sight of the pain pills on top of the latest true crime exploitation to climb the charts stopped him cold.

"Gabe? Is something wrong? Are you okay?"

In the shadows of Evangeline's living area, Gabe cradled the phone against his shoulder and tapped his finger against Evangeline's appointment calendar. One date was circled…the following Monday. And in the small box, she'd jotted an odd notation: J8.

"Everything's fine," he told his cousin Saura. "I just need to talk to John."

"Is it your mother—"

"No." She was on an Alaskan cruise. Then she would travel to France. She would be there until—

She'd be there until Gabe was certain the break-in at

her house had nothing to do with Gabe's crusade against Marcel Lambert. "She's safe."

"Thank God." The rustle of sheets, then the hush of whispers—Gabe didn't want to think about what he'd interrupted. It still blew his mind that his rough-around-the-edges police detective friend was about to marry his cousin.

When D'Ambrosia came onto the line, his voice was thick—*concerned.* "What did you find?"

Turning from the desk, Gabe slid the amber bottle into his pocket and did a quick survey of the room. He hadn't said a word to D'Ambrosia about looking into Marcel Lambert's role in Darci's life—or her death. But D'Ambrosia had his own way of finding things out.

"I need you to check something." Three steps brought Gabe to a curio cabinet, where he looked beyond artistically placed butterflies and photographs to the mirrored backing. There he saw what Evangeline must have seen in the warehouse, what the waitress had seen in the restaurant. What everyone had seen, John and Saura, the D.A. and the cop who'd pulled Gabe over for driving five miles under the speed limit at two in the morning.

It was all there, every perverted lie and sobering truth; every touch and every kiss, every footstep he'd thought he heard. Every file he thought was missing. Every pill.

Every mistake.

It was all there, blazing like a neon sign from eyes that had once been unreadable, carved into the lines of a face that had once been like granite. Like an open book, all those destructive shades of gray were there for anyone to read.

"About Evangeline," he said, and on a rough breath, closed the book. "Evangeline Rousseau."

* * *

The smell of coffee woke her. Once, the rich aroma would have made Evangeline smile and stretch, lazily wander toward the kitchen.

Now her heart slammed as it all rushed back, every damning detail—following Gabe into the warehouse, running through the shadows, the feel of his body plowing into hers. The feel of his legs straddling her and his hands against her arms, the dark expression when he'd recognized whom he'd pinned to the floor.

The wash of horror when he'd realized she was hurt.

She'd tried to get him to leave her alone. She'd told him she was fine. But he'd taken her to the free clinic anyway, stayed with her while the lady doctor examined her, taken her home once she was cleared.

And stayed.

Here.

On a cruel rush she swung to her feet, grabbed for the nightstand when the room tilted. Somehow she made her way to the door. And somehow she closed it, quietly. And turned the lock.

Then she was on the floor beside the bed and pulling out a fireproof box, fumbling with the combination lock and pulling it open as Simon crouched beside her.

Relief whispered in from all directions. She kneeled there in the hazy light, staring at…everything. They were all there, exactly as she'd left them. Every article. Every photograph. Every interview and theory and transcription.

With a deep breath, she lifted a hand and touched a finger to the picture of a young hotshot attorney, strolling from the courthouse after an improbable victory; his first. His suit had been dark gray, she remembered.

In the picture, it looked black.

With the old tom her brother had rescued rubbing against her legs, Evangeline locked the box, slid it under the bed and stood, knew what she had to do.

She was turning toward the mirror when the small amber vial on top of the paperback stopped her. Pain pills, she remembered, as another memory shifted against the shadows of the night—Gabe standing beside her bed with the bottle in his hand, gazing at it the way a new father gazes at the tiny life entrusted to him, with a combination of awe…and terror.

No. The word ripped through her, but she reached for the bottle, anyway, and thumbed off the lid, stared at the small blue tablets. The label indicated twelve had been prescribed. Eight remained.

Briefly she closed her eyes, opened them a heartbeat later: she had no idea how many she'd taken.

It didn't matter, she told herself. Gabe didn't matter. It didn't matter if he was popping pills or drinking too much. And it didn't matter if he blamed her for what had gone down at the D.A.'s office. She'd done what she'd been asked to do. She had nothing to feel guilty for, not even a little bit. That was like being a little bit pregnant or a little bit dead. Either you were, or you weren't.

And she wasn't.

Whatever Gabe had gotten himself involved with was his doing, not hers.

In the mirror she found the edges of a bruise leaking from behind her bandage. Wincing, she turned and made her way toward Gabe and the opportunity she'd never thought to find again—but slammed straight into another memory.

Because of the coffee.

With each step she took she could see Jimmy, her

brother, as he'd been that last morning, when she'd found him in the kitchen with his back to her, wearing only a pair of faded jeans as he'd looked out at the willow beyond the window. There'd been wind chimes hanging from the low branch. Ceramic flowers. She'd made them; he'd hung them. And he'd said when the wind whispered through them, it was the sound of angels.

He'd always been poetic like that.

He'd turned to her and smiled, held out an arm and drew her to his side. He'd promised everything would be okay.

A week later he'd been in prison for murder.

Sometimes it felt as if only a few days had passed since that muggy summer morning. In the twelve years since then, she'd seen him only a handful of times, and she'd never again awakened to the scent of fresh-brewed coffee. There'd been no more standing in that window.

And they'd never listened to the angels.

Throat tightening, she savored the anticipation. Jimmy wasn't waiting in the kitchen, but the man who'd taught her what it took to win—and what happened when you lost—was.

The sound of a morning news show drew her. It was Wednesday. With one very big exception over the weekend—a charity event involving none other than Marcel Lambert—her calendar was clear until Monday. She did need to make an appearance at the office—but even more, she needed to confirm her suspicions about just how far Gabriel Fontenot would go to make sure he always, always came out on top.

She found him standing in front of her old curio cabinet, with a pink pottery mug in one hand and a well-worn baseball in the other. And, for a moment, everything inside of her stopped. The punch came next, the distorted irony of seeing what had once been her brother's future in Gabriel Fontenot's deceptively well-manicured hands.

"You're still here," she said. And if her voice sounded too thick, she at least had the defense of sleep to fall back on.

He turned toward her, all rumpled six foot two of him, and frowned. "I told you I wasn't leaving you."

They were just words. She knew that. Throw aways. Meaningless. Chosen with care and delivered with skill, just like everything Gabriel Fontenot did.

Everything.

Before she could stop it, she remembered Gabe in his office and the look in his eyes, the feel of his mouth and the taste of his kiss, the desperation and the need and the—

Blocking the image, she destroyed it completely, but his words kept winding through her, sliding dangerously close to the place she could not allow him to touch—and, in doing so, reminded her why she had to be brutally careful with this man.

On more than one occasion she'd imagined a moment like this, Gabriel Fontenot in her loft, casual and comfortable and relaxed. This was what she'd wanted when she'd come to New Orleans, one-on-one time with him. Time to learn about each other. Time to build trust. To confide.

But she had no road map for this, no contingency plan for facing a man the morning after he'd caught her following him through a darkened warehouse. No guidelines for greeting the man who'd given her a concussion one moment then cradled her in his arms the next, who'd stayed by her side and watched over her.

Who watched her now.

And for the first time since he'd discovered her role in the D.A.'s sting, she would have sworn she didn't see contempt glittering in his eyes.

Maybe she was still groggy from the fall. Maybe she had some sort of hangover from the concussion. But the sight of him, his coffee-brown hair damp from a shower and curling at his nape, the grungy clothes from the night before gone, replaced by the faded jeans that fit a little too well and the white T-shirt he'd picked up from his house after leaving the clinic, came dangerously close to making her forget why she'd followed him to the warehouse in the first place—and what still had to be done.

"Thank you." Those were the right words. Her chest tightened, but she did not allow herself to look away, not while Gabe watched her so closely. Not while he held Jimmy's baseball. Her desk was locked, her laptop password protected. There was nothing lying around. She was more careful than that. He may have spent the night, but he hadn't found anything.

But he had tried. She knew that, too.

For over three months there'd been nothing. After learning she'd been feeding him false information with the sole intent of seeing if it went any further, he'd frozen her out of his life, made it clear he wanted nothing to do with her. That he stood here now, barefoot with a cup of coffee in his hand… It was a gift-wrapped opportunity she'd never expected. But wasn't about to turn away.

Even if that meant resurrecting the eight-hundred-pound gorilla sitting between them.

"I know this is the last place you want to be," she said, and if she'd had any doubt that while she slept, something had changed, the way Gabe continued to stand there so casually, looking at her with the discovery of a man who'd just made love to a woman for the first time, put a quick end to that.

"Not the last." Eyes glittering, he studied the baseball a heartbeat longer before returning it to the curio cabinet. Then, frowning, he stunned her by closing the distance between them.

His hand came next, slow and steady up to her face. His touch, excruciatingly gentle. "Dizzy?"

"No."

"No fresh blood," he said, lifting the edge of the bandage.

"I'm fine, really."

"This bruise isn't something you can hide," he warned, frowning. "There'll be questions."

"I know."

"The D.A. isn't going to like it."

In fact, he was going to hate it. Vincent Arceneaux made no secret of his political aspirations. Everything in his life was carefully engineered, from the clothes he wore to the woman he'd married, the home they lived in and the car he drove. His staff was no different. He demanded perfection.

A black eye was not perfection.

"I'll handle Vince," she said, realizing that Gabe's fate rested in her hands. She could tell the D.A. the truth, that she'd followed Gabe to a warehouse. Gabe, who was on leave, Gabe whose involvement in the case could result in a mistrial. The truth, the fact she'd caught him sneaking around, could slam an end to his career— and ensure Marcel Lambert's acquittal.

Lifting a hand, she eased Gabe's from her face. "I'll tell him I was mugged." The Gabriel Fontenot she knew would never ask, not the question, nor the favor. But she would cover for him, anyway, and in doing so, she would be one step closer to righting a very old wrong.

"Filing a false police report is against the law," he pointed out. "You could go to jail."

And she would definitely lose her job. "Let me worry about that."

Why? The question flickered in the cobalt of his eyes. Briefly. Then it was gone. Because they both knew the answer.

"Quid pro quo," he muttered.

Something for something. A favor for a favor. "No." Then, because she didn't understand what she saw in his eyes, she turned and walked into the kitchen, opened the cabinet and reached for a mug. Her throat tightened when she saw the alligator on the old chipped pottery, the name in a childish red font. Jimmy.

Hearing Gabe approach, she slid the mug to the back and reached for one that simply said Lawyers do it until justice prevails.

"It's Wednesday," she said, reaching for the coffeepot. "The month is March." She poured. "My name is Evangeline. You're Gabe." After returning the pot to the burner, she turned to him, and reminded herself to breathe. Gabriel Fontenot had a way of making even a courtroom seem too small, the way he stood and the way he watched, the barely concealed sense of…containment.

Her kitchen didn't stand a chance. Even barefoot wearing a pair of faded jeans with his back against the wall, he dominated the small room.

"Hold up some fingers," she said, calling on one of the quirky little smiles she used when asking a witness a seemingly out-of-left-field question.

Gabe's eyes gleamed. Never looking away, he lifted his left hand and folded down his ring and middle finger.

"Three," she said, trying not to wonder why a man who spent his days in an office had such callused hands—and how in the world she could have missed that fact the night before. His palm was wide, square, his fingers long and thick. "Try again."

This time he lowered his pinkie, but lifted the middle finger.

"Three," she said again. Then, after rattling off the name of the president, the date of the next national election and the Saints' most recent draft pick, she smiled broadly. "See?" She brought the mug to her lips. "All better."

Vintage Gabe, the coffee was strong, deceptively smooth.

"Evie."

The nickname burned in ways the hot coffee never could. She lowered the mug and looked at him, felt her heart beat low and hard and deep. For years, she'd cringed when anyone called her Evie. It hadn't been their right, their place. Only one person had ever called her Evie. Hearing the name on anyone else's voice had been…wrong.

Until Gabe.

He'd only said it once, the night after he'd buried a friend—Evangeline still couldn't believe Detective Alec Prejean had turned up alive a few months later. But they hadn't known that then, hadn't known that he'd been thrown from the explosion. For Gabe there'd only been the sobering truth that he was the one who'd sent Alec to the warehouse. She'd found Gabe after the funeral alone in his office, with a bottle of whiskey and a moun-

tain of guilt. Against every scrap of better judgment,
she'd reached for him. *Evie,* he'd rasped, and in the
blind moments that had followed, she'd never felt more
needed in her life.

Then he'd torn away, walked away.

After that, he'd never called her Evie again. Until
now. He'd been silent since following her into the kitch-
en, had just stood and tracked her movements. Now
there was a thickness to his voice at complete odds with
the hard edge to his eyes. "Stop."

The single word came at her like a hammer, reminding her why defense attorneys hated going up against
this man. She felt herself wince, but refused to voice the
question: *Stop what?*

Remembering.

Second-guessing.

Wanting him to be someone other than who he was.

"This isn't a game," he said quietly. "Last night was
real. The warehouse was real."

And he was real. He'd been so last night when he'd
skimmed a finger over her face while he thought she was
sleeping, and he was real now, standing in her kitchen.
And he'd been real when he'd stood in the courtroom,
a rookie prosecutor angling to make a name for himself
by sending a twenty-year-old kid without a penny to his
name to prison, for a murder he hadn't committed.

"Trust me," she said, angling her chin. "I'm well
aware of that."

"You should never have followed me inside."

What she never should have done was forget.

"I could have hurt you a lot worse," he said, frowning
at the side of her face.

Automatically, she lifted a hand to finger the bandage.

He stepped closer and kept his eyes concentrated on her face. And though he didn't touch, she felt. This was…different. The way he was acting, the way he was looking at her.

"Go ahead," he said. "Ask."

The urge to step back was strong, the need to breathe without drawing in the scent of leather and sandalwood and man. *Of Gabe.* But she didn't let herself move, made herself tilt her chin and look up at him. "Ask what?"

"What I was doing there last night…why an A.D.A. on leave was at an abandoned warehouse at dusk."

All throughout her little receptors started to vibrate. She *had* wondered. That's why she'd followed him, to see if he was finally going to hand her the evidence she'd been craving since the hot afternoon she'd sat in stunned silence as the jury foreman had read a verdict there'd been no proof to support.

All these years later, her body still tightened at the memory—and the sight of the young attorney going out to celebrate, while her brother had been carted off to prison.

The sight of Gabe walking into the warehouse had simply confirmed what she'd known all along—that a technicality like being on leave wouldn't stop him from going after what he wanted. And for some reason, what he wanted was Marcel Lambert behind bars, regardless of due process or law or truth.

Reaching for her mug, she brought it to her mouth and took a long, bitter sip.

"You were there because of Marcel Lambert," she said as if it were the most natural answer in the world. Then she laid down her bluff. "You got the same tip I did."

His eyes went dark. "I didn't get a tip."

* * *

It wasn't easy to surprise Evangeline Rousseau. In the few months she'd been with the district attorney's office, she'd gained a reputation for thoroughness and tenacity. If there was a stone to be turned, she turned it. An angle to be played, she played it.

A shade of gray to be finessed, she finessed it.

Gabe looked at her now, at the quick flare of her eyes and felt the sweet curl of satisfaction. His blunt answer had surprised her. She'd given him an out he could easily have taken. Yes. He'd gotten the same tip she had. Someone had lured him to the warehouse on the promise of juicy information. End of story.

But Gabe wasn't ready for this story to end, not so long as Marcel Lambert's fate rested in Evangeline's hands. Even if that meant he had to hold those hands to make sure Lambert paid for his crimes.

"Then, what?" She took a long slow sip before continuing. "You were the *something interesting* I was supposed to find? Someone knew you were going to be there and deliberately set me up to find you?"

The same someone who'd stolen his files. "Which you did."

She shifted, allowing the brown hair to fall into her face. "But why me? If someone wanted you out of the way—"

"Not *if.*" Someone definitely wanted him out of the way—and out of the D.A.'s office. He wasn't imagining things. It wasn't the whiskey or the pain pills. He was definitely being followed. A locksmith had verified that his dead bolt had been jimmied.

"You have Arceneaux's ear," he pointed out, though it was hard to believe at the moment. Wearing a huge gray New Orleans Saints T-shirt hanging to her knees, her toenails decorated with small pink flowers, her hair uncombed and her face scrubbed clean, she looked more like a coed than a cutthroat attorney.

Val had—

Val.

Christ. Val had possessed the same ability.

"The D.A. relies on you," he said, "trusts you to warn him of situations that could taint his office. All you have to do is tell him what you found—" he tried to look at the ugly bruise leaking from behind the bandage…the bruise *he'd* put there "—where I was."

He could still feel her beneath him, the brutal stab of awareness when he'd realized whom he'd driven to the ground.

Biting down on her lower lip, she pushed past him and crossed to the far side of the kitchen—which wasn't that far—putting as much space between them as possible. Which again, wasn't that much. "Wouldn't it make more sense for our anonymous tipster to call the D.A. directly?"

She had fresh flowers on the small round table— nothing fancy, just the grocery-store kind. The table was dark and distressed, maybe an antique, but far more likely from the flea market. In one neat little stack she had three catalogs and four magazines. He'd thumbed through them all the night before.

"Depends on the game being played," he said, watching her set the mug on top of the newsmagazine. Games, after all, were her specialty. "It would have been more straightforward to call Vince, yes." But straightforward wasn't how Marcel Lambert played. "Except, now they've got you as well as me."

He saw the exact moment recognition struck. "You think someone set us up."

The only question was whether she was involved, or truly an innocent bystander. "Someone knew exactly how each of us would act," he said, crossing to the table. His money was on Lambert. "That your presence would destroy my meet." He spun one of the two chairs around and straddled it. "That you would stop me, but your guilt wouldn't let you turn me in. Then they would own us both."

And in doing so, someone had all but gift wrapped the opportunity Gabe had been looking for. If Evangeline's need for penance led her to keep quiet, then he, in turn, had just as much leverage over her as she did over him.

Her hands curved around the back of the other chair, but she did not sit. She looked beyond him toward the small window where a set of wind chimes hung from a plant hook. Ceramic flowers. He didn't need to turn around to see them. He knew they were there. He knew how many cans of Diet Coke were in her refrigerator, and that she had a weakness for graham crackers.

A man could learn a lot about a woman while she slept.

"Why risk tampering with a jury," he pointed out when she continued to say nothing, "when you can tamper with the prosecutors? Bait a trap and wind them up; put them on a collision course."

The heater rattled on as she turned back to him with steel in her gaze. "There's just one problem with that theory. No one owns me."

Her bravado served her well in the courtroom. It would serve him well, too.

"Then call the D.A." Pulling the phone from his waistband, he slid it across the table. "If you don't—"

"I'm not calling Vince." With the words, she slid the hair from her face and, damn it, everything inside him

tightened. Because he could see more of the bruise—
and because she'd called the D.A. by his first name.
There'd been dinners. She'd been seen laughing with
the D.A.'s wife at one of Lambert's charity auctions.
"If someone wants to play, let them. But I won't be
manipulated—and I'm not hanging you out to dry."

Again.

The unspoken word echoed through the silence.

He stood. "Be very sure, Evangeline." The words
were quiet—deceptively soft. "Know who you're crawling into bed with—and why."

Her eyes, the color of the storm clouds that liked to
hover over the Gulf, met his. "The past can't be undone,
Gabe. What happened with Val can't be erased. Trust
me, I know that."

The words were equally quiet, but they slammed
into him with the force of one of those afternoon storms.
He didn't want that from her. He didn't want quiet. He
didn't want to look into her eyes and see regret…or
compassion.

"I'm not calling Vince," she said again, and even
though she wore that ridiculously big T-shirt, the fierce
angle of her chin reminded him of the way he'd once
seen her go head-to-head with a slimy ambulance
chaser. "If you want to turn this into a game, fine, go
ahead. Threaten me. Call him, yourself, if you like, tell
him my dirty little secret, that I found you trespassing
into my case but didn't turn you in. Do it. Enjoy it—
that's your decision. I've made mine."

The thrill of the hunt pulsed deeper. There was
no turning back, he knew. No time for second-guessing
decisions. Evangeline knew the rules, the stakes. She'd
made her bed, all but invited him in.

He'd be a fool to ignore the opportunity. He'd take what she offered and get what he wanted. He'd right a wrong. He'd taste justice.

And then he would walk away. And not look back.

Because guilt, he knew, made people far too careless.

"Tell me about Wild Berry," he said, rocking forward on the chair's legs. "Did you get a tip to go there, too?"

She tensed. "Come again?"

With a nod he gestured toward the living room, where her small desk sat by the window. "Your calendar." He'd felt like a son of a bitch when he'd put his hand to the file drawers. But then he'd seen his sister through the darkness of his mind. Camille, wet and scared, twelve years old and cradled in his best friend's arms. Jack had been the one to find her after she'd turned up missing— after their father had been found dead.

Suicide, the coroner said. A single gunshot to the head.

Camille'd said different. She'd said there'd been a second man in the room with her father....

Her accusation had been all Gabe needed to give Evangeline's file drawer a solid pull. Whatever information she'd amassed against Marcel Lambert, whatever evidence...

The drawer had been locked, her computer password protected. "I saw it when I was looking for a piece of paper. You're going there, aren't you? To Darci's hometown."

Suspicion lit Evangeline's eyes. He could tell she didn't buy his story, but she'd also just vowed she wasn't going to turn on him.

Frowning, she walked toward the sink, picked up a small glass and filled it with tap water. "She was nineteen years old, Gabe." And finally, finally, she sounded like the Evangeline he'd first met, the colleague who'd sometimes propped a hip on the corner of his desk to discuss the nuances of law.

"A kid," she said as if she'd known Darci somehow. Leaning forward, Evangeline put her hand to the flowers and pushed them back from the edge of the vase, then poured the water from the glass. "She'd only been in New Orleans a few months. How does that happen? How did she—"

"How did she what?" He'd seen the crime-scene photos. Darci had been a pretty girl. She'd had a mother and a father, a goldfish. She'd collected magnets. "Meet Marcel Lambert?" Gabe had seen the two of them together, only days before Darci was killed. The bastard had brought the girl into his own house, right under his wife's nose. "Become his mistress?"

Evangeline stared at the flowers. "Get herself murdered."

One little mistake, that's all it took. Giving trust to someone who didn't deserve it. Letting your emotions trump caution. "She met Marcel Lambert…became his mistress."

Evangeline shifted to brace her hip against the side of the old table. "You want it to be him, don't you?" There was no accusation in the question; only understanding—and a dull blade of curiosity. "That's why you can't let this case go, because you want to make sure Marcel falls."

"That's a prosecutor's job. To prosecute."

"You make it sound so black-and-white."

"Either someone is guilty, or they're not."

"What if Marcel isn't?" Evangeline asked as she set the empty glass onto the table.

It was a logical question, the kind any good prosecutor had to ask. Cover every possible angle. Evaluate every scenario. Turn over every stone the defense might throw. Gabe knew that. But if Lambert was innocent, if someone else killed Darci—

It would be more than just a case that he lost.

"Something doesn't feel right," Evangeline said. She eased away from the table and crossed the kitchen, leaned against an empty corkboard, all but piercing him with her gaze. "It's too neat and tidy. Rich, powerful man. Poor, desperate girl. A sordid affair. A tragic ending."

She made it sound like one of those Cameron Monroe true-crime books his cousin Saura insisted that he read.

"I want to know *her.*" Evangeline's T-shirt rode high against her thighs in a way her tailored suits had never done. "I want to know the girl she was before she came to New Orleans. I want to know what made her tick and what made her cry. What she wanted…"

Gabe stood. "And who else might have wanted her dead."

"If there is someone else, yes."

"Do you really think it's that easy? You just stroll down to Wild Berry and ask a few questions, find out everything you want to know?" The cops had already conducted their investigation. And unlike all those years ago, this time all roads led in the same direction. "Say you stumble across some big secret, some other reason why Darci called a police detective the night before she was murdered." She'd been scared. D'Ambrosia had heard it in her voice. "You really think someone's just going to let you find that information?"

Evangeline lifted her chin. "What are you saying?"

She was a professional. She knew how to handle

herself, how to take care of herself. She'd prosecuted monsters before. And, yet, the thought of her poking around in Darci's secrets made something inside Gabe twist. Lambert would not sit back and let Evangeline Rousseau—let anyone—take him down.

He'd take first.

"Darci was murdered," Gabe and his voice was rougher than he'd intended. "What do you think that someone will do to make sure you don't prove by whom?"

Evangeline wasn't a woman to look away or back down. Even when she should. Standing there in the hazy light, she looked at him as if he was warning her about something as mundane as getting out of bed. "It's my job—and I don't run scared."

"Maybe you should."

"Gabe." Her voice was oddly quiet. "Stop."

"Stop what?"

"This." She gestured toward him with her arm. "Standing here in my kitchen like you care, like you're concerned." She swallowed and looked away, stared hard at the little flower wind chimes. "I'm not stupid," she said in a voice that brought acid to his chest. "I'm not naive. I know none of this is real."

He wouldn't let himself move, sure as hell wouldn't let himself walk toward her. Because she was right. None of this was real. None. Of. It.

She turned back to him. "You want something," she added, softer this time, but with a precision that pierced. "And it's not me."

Chapter 3

Gabe didn't move.

"This is me, Gabe," she said, shoving the hair from her face. "I'm not stupid. I know how you feel about me…which is why I know better than to believe it's me you're really concerned about. This is about him, isn't it? Marcel."

The muscle in the hollow of his cheek started to pound.

"You want to see him fall. You want to be the one to push him. But tell me something, Gabe," she pressed, and the gray of her eyes went oddly dark. "Just how far are you willing to go to make that happen?"

In another situation he might have smiled. Hazy morning light played against her face, giving her the girl-next-door glow that made her so lethal in the courtroom.

"You really think I'm concerned about limits?" he asked mildly.

He would have sworn it was disappointment that flashed through her gaze. "But what if he's *innocent?*" she asked again.

It almost sounded as if she wanted him to be. "What if he's not?"

Her eyes met his. "Then, he'll be convicted."

"You really think it works like that, all nice and tidy? That justice comes with a pretty bow wrapped around it?"

"No." It was barely a whisper. "But his record is clean," she said, and then she was moving again, looking tall and regal and composed despite her bare legs and the flowers on her toenails.

"He's a respected member of the community," she went on, brushing by him and reaching for a small shelf beside the table. "Walk into almost any home in this state and you'll find one of his cookbooks." To demonstrate, she pulled one from her own shelf. "You think a jury is going to send him to Angola on circumstantial evidence alone?"

No. He didn't need to be an A.D.A to know that. Only a boy. A son. The Lamberts were slippery. They had money and influence and charm. Without concrete evidence, Marcel would get away with murder—again.

Taking the cookbook from her hands, he flipped open the back cover and stared at the man's ruddy cheeks and salt-and-pepper hair, the self-satisfied gleam in his eyes. Black was black and white was white. There could be no shades of gray—not with this man and not with this woman.

No matter how badly Gabe had once wished that there were.

"There will be more than circumstantial evidence." He raised his gaze to Evangeline's. "That's why I'm going with you."

For the second time in less than an hour, he suc-
ceeded in surprising her. "Come again?"

"To Wild Berry," he said, and though he kept his
face expressionless, inside he savored the hand of aces.
"The sheriff is a friend of mine, Jack Savoie." But not
even his badge was yielding the answers they needed.
Folks didn't want to talk about Darci Falgoust—or
Marcel Lambert. Especially to the law. "He'll run in-
terference."

"We." She enunciated the word distinctly, as if it
were a foreign concept to be studied and dissected.

"You can tell me no," he said, tossing the cookbook
onto the table. "You can get up tomorrow and drive
down there, but when you arrive, I'll already be there."
Looking for proof that Darci and Marcel had been involved. "I'll already have the doors open."

"And you'll make sure they close for me," she said
with a quiet that had nothing to do with defeat. "Gabe."
Her voice thickened on his name. "We're on the same
side. We want the same thing."

He doubted that. "Then, don't force my hand."

For a long moment she said nothing, just looked at
him with the oddest light glowing in her eyes. Gray,
damn it. Even standing beneath the fluorescent light of
the kitchen, with the light of the sun falling on her, her
eyes were still gray.

And like one of those flowers that his uncle had always warned him not to touch, she still fascinated.

"There's more to this than you're telling me," she said.

From the moment he'd turned around to see her
emerging from the hall, he'd deliberately kept his distance. There'd been enough touching the night before.
But now he allowed himself to move, to feather a single

finger against the bandage at her temple. "With us, there always is."

The rusted remains of an old sugar mill hulked over Wild Berry like a worn-out landlord. To the left of the town's only stop sign sat Ardoin's Tractor and Feed; to the right, Bonaventure's Landing. The small country grocery and smokehouse looked nondescript and run-down on the outside and not a whole lot better on the inside.

The smell of grease and pepper permeated the old building, courtesy of years of fried shrimp and catfish, of étouffé and gumbo and jambalaya and boudin.

"So, you two are newlyweds?" the owner, Rosemunde, asked as she reached beside a stack of pecan pies for two menus.

With a lazy grin, Gabe slid an arm around Evangeline and pulled her to his side. "I got me a pretty one, didn't I?"

"Almost three months," Evangeline added. Then, for the shock value of it, she slid a hand to cup her stomach. As much as she hated the feel of his hand on her body, his idea that they pose as a young married couple was inspired. The people of Wild Berry weren't talking to the law. But a young couple just passing through… Harmless.

"Mama thought it best if we hitched up before I start showing."

Against her hip, Gabe's hand tensed—the pregnancy bit had not been part of the plan. At least, not *his* plan. But classic Gabe, his face gave away nothing. He gazed down at her with one of those slow, black-magic smiles, then pressed a kiss to the top of her nose. "I'm hoping for a girl," he said, not missing a beat. "As pretty as her mama."

Rosemunde clasped her hands together. "How wonderful."

"'Course, the way she's eating," Gabe drawled in rare form, "she might have a whole litter in there."

It shouldn't have been possible. Only four months had passed since she'd last been this close to Gabe. And in those four months she'd never been far away. But somehow she *had* forgotten. She'd forgotten what it was like to have him touch her—and how easily he could manipulate a situation to get what he wanted.

"Now, Russell Rae, you stop that," she said, playing along. "You know I've only gained two little pounds."

"So you keep telling me," he said, sliding his hand from her hip to her stomach. "But I can already feel—"

She swatted him, didn't want him to touch any more intimately than he already had. "How many times do I have to tell you, there will be no feeling in public?"

A dark light glowed in Gabe's eyes as he retrieved his hand.

Laughing, Rosemunde led them toward a booth against the window opening to the parking lot. "Mornin' rush is over," she said. "The lunch folks will be in soon. But, until then, you kids have the place mostly to yourselves." She placed the laminated menus on the table then gestured for Evangeline to slide in. "Get you some juice or coffee, hon?"

"Coffee'd be great," Evangeline said out of habit, but then Gabe slid in beside her and stretched an arm behind her shoulders.

"Make that a decaf," he instructed. "Save the real stuff for me. And orange juice," he added. "For both of us. Mama says our little lima bean needs plenty of folic acid."

Rosemunde nodded. "I'll be back for your order in a sec." Smiling like a proud aunt, she turned and strolled toward the counter, where two older men sat on barstools.

"Lima bean?" Evangeline lifted a brow. *"Folic acid?"*

Gabe just gave her a lazy grin, as if the two of them sat hip to hip in a backwater diner every morning—and he'd never caught her putting a knife into his back. "Inspired, wasn't it?"

His voice was low, relaxed, the Gabe from before, not the man who manipulated juries and card games, but the man who would kick off his shoes and prop his socked feet on his desk, flip on the stereo behind him and sing the blues.

She'd forgotten what that voice could do to her.

But she hadn't forgotten what Gabe could do. What he *had* done.

It was as though a switch had been flipped—on or off, she didn't know. He wore a pair of faded jeans like the ones she'd found him in the morning before. He'd chosen an ivory button-down, wrinkled with the sleeves rolled up, the tail untucked. His hair was combed, but whiskers shadowed his jaw. On his feet he wore scuffed cowboy boots. On his wrist, a cheap, digital watch.

Looking at him, Rosemunde would never guess that this man possessed one of Louisiana's brightest legal minds. That there were those who'd wanted him to run for lieutenant governor.

He just looked like…like Russell Rae, an easygoing Southern man out for breakfast with his pregnant, pony-tailed wife.

But Evangeline knew. She knew who he was and what he'd done, what she'd done to him. She knew about the pills, and as she slid a glance his way, she saw the shadows in his eyes that he would never allow Rosemunde to see. That he didn't want Evangeline to see.

"What strikes your fancy, sugar?" he asked, relaxing the hand pressed to her shoulder. "I hear their andouille is legendary."

Who was this man? she wondered in some faraway corner of her mind. Who was this man who could prowl through her apartment one morning, making the small space feel more like a holding cell than the sanctuary it had been, only to sprawl in a booth beside her the next morning and shoot the breeze as if there was nowhere else in the world he wanted to be.

The answer tightened through her.

He was a player. He could be anyone, hide anything. It's what made him so good and so dangerous.

"Bacon," she said with her own smitten smile. "Crispy-fried." Then she nudged against his thigh. "Scooch over, darlin'. I need to powder my nose."

With a long, measured look, he did as she asked and let her slide across the torn red vinyl. She'd taken four steps before he spoke. "Grits or hash browns?"

That was easy. "Surprise me," she said, twisting around and meeting his eyes. "It's what you do best."

Gabe watched her go. The gypsy-style top took at least ten years off her. With the short ponytail and minimal makeup, the hip-hugging jeans, she could easily pass for some man's young, innocent bride. She'd no sooner cleared the door to the ladies' room than Rosamunde was at his side taking their orders.

Jack hadn't called. His friend was downplaying it, but Gabe knew Jack had heard the rumors, too, about someone asking a whole lot of questions that no one wanted to answer. They'd been friends since they claimed the same fishing hole as six-year-olds. Gabe had been there when Jack's mama was diagnosed with breast cancer just as Jack had when Gabe's mother's scream had jolted the boys from a late-night game of cards. War, Gabe remembered. He'd been winning.

"Gabe?"

He twisted toward the quiet voice and saw her standing there, not the woman he'd first met in the courthouse cafeteria all those months ago, the woman whose ability to bluff he'd never even suspected. He saw Lilah Mae, the casually dressed woman with shiny lip gloss and a fake tattoo inside her wrist, looking at him with the dread of a wife whose husband had just hung up the phone from bad news.

"Everything okay?" she asked.

He hadn't said a word. He wasn't even looking at her. He was looking out the window, at the sign advertising the lunch special. But somehow she saw. And somehow she knew.

The way she had before.

Once her ability to read him had fascinated. Only a select handful had been able to—his cousins Cain and Saura, his friend Jack. His sister. All of them were people he trusted. And loved. Who loved him back.

And then there was Evangeline.

"Well, now, Lilah, darlin'," he drawled, finding the unaffected grin of Russell Rae. He slid from the booth and gestured for her to return to her spot by the window, where a child's handprint remained. "'Course everything's okay. Why wouldn't it be?"

Toward the front, the bell on the door jingled, but he

didn't look away from Evangeline—or the flash of longing he thought he saw in her eyes.

"I just thought…you looked upset," she said, easing
around him and reclaiming her seat. "I thought maybe
Jack had called, that there was news."

He lowered himself back into the booth. "No news."

She glanced toward the kitchen, then back at him. "A
couple of young women just got here," she said. "Probably
a few years older than Darci. One of them is pregnant."

With a nod, Gabe reached for his coffee and took a
long bitter sip.

"Ga—*Russell*," she corrected, quieter this time, and
then her hand was on his, soft and intimate. Familiar.
"If it's your head, I've got some aspirin—"

"I don't need pills." Didn't want them. He pulled his
hand from hers and put the mug back on the table, trying
damn hard not to slam it.

"Maybe a massage then," she said, angling toward
him and lifting her hands. Her fingers found his temple,
and caressed.

Don't. The word flashed, even as the pressure of her
fingertips sent little waves of pleasure eddying through
him. "My head is fine," he said, but before he could pull
away, he saw Rosemunde strolling toward them with a
tray balanced on her hand. "But you sure do know what
you're doing, sugarplum," he drawled. "I am a lucky
man to get for free what a lot of people charge for."

The innuendo flew right by Rosemunde, who sidled
up beside them and began unloading plates, but
Evangeline's mouth tightened.

"Got you some grits here," Rosemunde said, placing
the large ceramic bowl in front of her. "Your husband
had me add some cheese as a surprise."

"That was right nice of you," Evangeline said, but her voice was different now, strained. Almost…hurt. "Russell's always had a way of surprising me."

"Something tells me he's good at it, too," Rosemunde said, laughing.

Gabe lifted his eyes to Evangeline's. "Just want my girl to get what she deserves."

Rosemunde placed a plate of powdered-sugar-covered French toast between them. "You sure did get yourself a good one, hon—he got any brothers?" Laughing, she winked. "Or maybe an uncle…"

The words hit a little too close. Bayou de Foi wasn't that far from Wild Berry—he had no doubt Rosemunde not only knew of his family, but of his uncles, the senator and the sheriff. Both had reputations. Both had broken more than one heart.

"None good enough for you," he drawled.

"Everything looks just wonderful." Evangeline diverted their waitress. With her hand to his thigh she gave a little squeeze, signaling that she was about to go fishing. "I have to say, you are every bit as sweet as Darci said you were."

The change was immediate—in Evangeline, who let her voice trail off and her gaze lower, and in Rosemunde, who stopped laughing. Stopped smiling. Maybe even breathing.

"Who?" Her voice was different, too; wooden almost. Scraped raw.

Watchful, Gabe slid an arm around Evangeline as she explained. "Darci Falgoust." Her smile was purposefully sad. "You do know her, don't you? She said she was from here, talked about you and The Landing all the time."

It was a leap, but one they had to take. Gabe knew small towns. Deli-marts were gathering spots, their owners figures in everyone's lives. Darci had even worked here; D'Ambrosia had confirmed that. It only served to reason that she and Rosemunde had shared a relationship.

The older woman suddenly looked every year of her age. "You knew Darci Faye?" The words were no more than a broken whisper.

"Worked with her in N'Awlins," Evangeline said, frowning. "She was always telling me I needed to come to Wild Berry and see for myself how a restaurant should be run."

Rosemunde's eyes went disturbingly hard.

"I still can't believe she's gone," Evangeline continued when Rosemunde said nothing. She was good, convincing. If he hadn't known better, he would have actually believed she'd known the young woman, had cared about her.

But this time he did know better.

"She was…" When her words trailed off, Gabe gathered Evangeline close and lifted a hand to her face.

"You okay, darlin'?"

Her eyes, deep and dark and touched by a sadness that looked oddly real, met his. "I will be." The words were quiet, wistful. "But Darci won't. And it's just so wrong. I mean, why would Marcel want to hurt her? She loved him—and he loved her. It just doesn't make any sense."

Gabe feathered a finger along her cheekbone as Rosemunde paled. Evangeline didn't know the Lamberts. Gabe did, and he suspected the restaurant owner did, too.

"Things don't always make sense, child," she said.

"Sometimes it's best just to accept that." Then she turned and walked away.

Gabe pulled Evangeline into his arms and held her, pretended to console her. "Let me watch." He felt the tension in her body, even as she settled against his chest, the scent of powder and vanilla drifting from her hair.

Because he wanted to bury his face, he forced himself to look away.

"She's at the bar," he narrated quietly. "Talking with those two men." He saw one of them tense, the second reach for his mobile phone. "Now she's going back into the kitchen."

Evangeline started to lift her head, but he tangled a hand in her hair and eased her back against him, felt the rise and fall of her chest, the warmth of her breath against the open collar of his shirt. And when one of the men glanced their way, he lowered his face to Evangeline's and pressed a soft kiss to her temple. "One of them's watching," he explained with another little kiss. This one slower. "Doesn't look pleased."

Evangeline slid a hand to cup his face and pulled back, looked at him. The look in her eyes was softer than he'd seen in weeks. "Did you catch the way Rosemunde changed?"

"Either she knows something or she's scared," he said, wiping the nonexistent tears from her face with a brush of his thumb.

Evangeline's eyes closed for a long, damning moment. "Or both."

"Or both," he agreed as the jingle of the bell announced the arrival of two more men, not casually dressed like everyone else, but in dark sunglasses and gray suits. "We've got more friends," he whispered, and

Evangeline cut her gaze toward the small lobby, where one of the two veered toward the kitchen.

"What is it they say about lawyers and rats?" Evangeline's voice was dry, but the amusement leaked through.

"Give them a crumb," Gabe muttered.

"Or a paycheck," she added with a fleeting smile. "Who do you think they are?"

"No telling. Could be local, or could be Marcel's." Standing guard and making sure no one blabbed. Which meant there was definitely something *to* blab.

Realizing they'd fallen out of their guise, Gabe returned his hand to smooth Evangeline's hair. "I'll ask Jack."

He would have sworn she tilted into his touch. "Or they could work for someone else…someone who has something to hide."

Gabe worked hard not to frown.

"Don't you think it's odd," she added, "that all I did was mention Darci's name, and everyone went on lockdown?"

He let a finger graze her mouth. "We'd probably better start eating."

"You didn't answer my question," she said as she picked up her fork.

"I didn't think I needed to."

The bell on the door announced the arrival of three older women. Early forties, Gabe guessed. One of them used crutches. Rosemunde met them and they all shot a quick glance toward Evangeline and Gabe before taking a table halfway across the restaurant.

Gabe knew pressure. He knew intensity. He knew anticipation. He lived it every day in the courtroom, during voir dire, when attorneys from both sides underwent the pivotal process of selecting a jury. During opening arguments, when the courtroom would fall to a hush as the prosecutor and the defense laid out their arguments. During testimony, when the defendant took the stand. When a surprise witness made an appearance, or a piece of evidence backfired.

He knew those moments, the waiting, when every second stretched like an eternity as an invisible cord wound tight, when the silence screamed. He knew and he craved.

"You feel it, too," Evangeline whispered, but he didn't look at her, didn't want to see her eyes. He heard enough in her voice, the quiet understanding, the subtle affirmation. Because he did feel it, everything, the taut veil of fear gripping The Landing, the hush and the waiting, the curiosity and the dread and the anticipation, but more than just the tension, he felt the craving, too. Deep inside. Here, in some stupid backwater diner, with her. *Evangeline.*

And for the first time since he'd held Val in his arms as she took her last breath, something strong and vital and alive coiled through him. This, he knew. Finding the truth, chasing down justice. It wasn't just what he was supposed to do. It was who he was.

"One of the suits is coming," Evangeline whispered as he lowered his mug. Slowly, with a casualness he didn't come close to feeling, he twisted as the taller of the two approached. "Mornin'," he drawled, "can I help you with something?"

The man, with short dark hair and an expensively cut suit, slid off his sunglasses and looked past Gabe toward Evangeline. "You the gal who worked with Darci?"

In an act of sheer brilliance, she put a protective hand to her stomach. "Yes."

The man's lean face revealed a hollow beneath his

sharp cheekbone. "That girl hurt a lot of people when she left town…even more when she got herself killed."

Instinctively Gabe urged Evangeline closer.

"I can only imagine," she whispered. "I'm so sorry."

His expression remained like granite. "If you're looking to reminisce about your friend, you've come to the wrong place."

The obvious scare tactic landed with the pure beauty of a hand of aces. This, Gabe knew, was why he'd insisted on coming. "Easy there," he said, taking over. "We're not looking for *any*thing."

"Then perhaps you should be on your way," the man said, reaching inside his suit coat.

Three seconds, that's all that could have passed. But in them the diner flashed away and Gabe remembered, the subtle movement and the gun, the split second between life and death. The explosion and the sound of gunfire, Val falling. It was something dark and primal that pushed him to his feet to shield Evangeline, even as the other man extracted a simple leather wallet.

Everything inside of Gabe stilled.

"Maybe this will help…" The man flipped open the wallet and thumbed out several bills. Hundreds. All of them crisp. New.

They landed next to Gabe's coffee mug.

"Oh, my," Evangeline breathed in sheer perfection from behind him, and the sudden desire to pull her into his arms and kiss her hard rocked him.

"We don't need your money," Gabe growled, but the man in the Armani suit was already striding toward Rosemunde. She glanced from him to Gabe and Evangeline, then back to the man and nodded. Then she made her way toward them, while the two men, who so clearly didn't belong, watched.

"I hear you're ready for your check," she said in an odd, whitewashed voice. But her eyes were dark, on edge.

"Rosemunde." Behind him, Gabe felt Evangeline move. She stood, pushed past him and made her way toward the older woman. "I—I'm so sorry… I didn't mean to make trouble." She reached for Rosemunde's hand, just as she'd reached for Gabe's that very first day. Except she didn't shake. She clasped. "I just…I just wanted to come here, to feel close to Darci again."

The natural color had not returned to Rosemunde's face, leaving two garish slashes of blush and lips the color of faded peaches. "Then, go." With the whisper, she pulled her hand from Evangeline's. *"Please."* Turning to Gabe, she handed him the bill. "If you really were a friend of Darci's, that's what you'll do. And you won't come back."

Terror. It was an emotion Gabe recognized too easily—the corrosive force of it vibrated from every line of Rosemunde's ample body. The woman wasn't just scared, she was terrified.

"This was a mistake," Evangeline whispered, turning from Rosemunde to take the check from Gabe's hands. She glanced at it, opened her purse and pulled out a twenty, slapped it down on the table next to the stack of one hundreds, then looked up at him. "I don't like this place," she said in the soft, sincere voice of Lilah Mae— the voice he'd sometimes heard at night when he closed his eyes. "We should never have come here."

Taking her cue, he slid his arm around her waist and pulled her close. "We shouldn't have done a lot of things." Then, while the silence echoed and everyone in the diner watched, Russell Rae pressed a tender kiss to the top of his wife's head and led her out the door. Evangeline leaned into him and wrapped her arms around his middle, walking nothing at all like a fearless attorney taking the courtroom, but with the relaxation and contentment of a woman with the man she trusted.

It was a hell of a powerful illusion.

The beat-up white pickup he'd borrowed that morning waited outside—his new SUV, they'd agreed, would have been a dead giveaway. He opened the door and helped her in, then rounded the front, turning back toward the country grocery one last time. The two men in sunglasses stood outside the double doors, watching. He looked their way for a long, hard moment, then slid behind the steering wheel and started the engine, heard the crunch of gravel as they backed toward the two-lane highway.

He wondered if Jack had any idea what the hell was going on in this allegedly no-account town on the far side of his parish.

Cypress and oak crowded the side of the bumpy road, their canopies thinner than normal thanks to a drier-than-average winter, but still blotting out most of the sun.

"Maybe it *is* Marcel," Evangeline said as he accelerated into a sharp curve and passed a makeshift cross marking the spot where Jack's wife had died. Glancing toward her, he fully expected to see the hard-nosed attorney sitting next to him, because that's whose voice he heard: sharp and intelligent, suspicious. But it was Lilah he saw, the ponytail making her eyes look too big and too dark for her face, the lip gloss she'd reapplied and the wistful gypsy shirt. In her hand she held a crumpled piece of paper.

"Or maybe it's someone else," she was saying. "But someone has put the fear of God into this town."

The substandard road, still scarred from Katrina's battering and nine straight days of stagnant floodwater, wound deep into the heavily wooded area in the heart of Jack's parish—and closer to memories Gabe had no desire to visit.

"Murder will do that," he muttered. "She was one of their own. That's never easy." The image flashed before he could stop it, Camille, her straight blond hair and grass-green eyes, the freckles over her nose.

His sister had been right, damn it. She'd been right. *About everything.*

Beside him, Evangeline reached for the beaded purse with fringe dangling from its edges—he would never have even guessed she owned such a thing.

"There's a phone number," she said, pulling out her cell phone. "I'm going to call it."

Out of the corner of his eye he saw the bill in her lap—the one Rosemunde had pressed into his hand—and the phone number scrawled on the back. Two words: Please. Call.

"Let me," he started, swerving to avoid a pothole. "Russell Rae wouldn't want his wife—"

The single gunshot killed the rest of his words.

Chapter 4

"Hang on!"

The hard edge of Gabe's voice ripped through Evangeline. She grabbed for the handle above her head and held on as trees rushed up to greet them. Gabe had one hand on the steering wheel, the other reaching for her as the truck veered toward the canal.

Everything accelerated. Blurred. The narrow shoulder and the muddy water, the mob of trees closing around them. Her heart kicked hard but she didn't scream, couldn't scream. Couldn't do anything but stare at the vicious concentration in Gabe's eyes, the way he kept his hand steady on the wheel as the truck slowed, until it stopped, half on, half off the road.

"Son of a bitch," he growled, but then he was throwing the gear into Park and twisting toward her, lifting his hands to her body and running them along her blouse and jeans. "Christ God, are you okay?"

She blinked, tried to breathe. "I'm fine," she said, because she was. She hadn't been shot—he hadn't been shot. The truck seemed intact. "What just happened—"

He was already pulling away and throwing open the door, climbing out. She did the same, found him staring at the back right tire. "A blowout," she whispered.

With hard eyes he turned back toward The Landing and swore under his breath.

Maybe fictitious good ole boy Russell Rae would believe it was an accident, but Assistant District Attorney Gabriel Fontenot knew they'd just received their second warning.

"Gabe…" Maybe she shouldn't have touched him, but she wasn't thinking about anything other than the moment, the cold fury in his eyes and the violence of his stance.

"He won't get away with this," he said, pivoting to face her. "Russell Rae and Lilah were nobody. *Nobody.* No threat to *him.*" A surprisingly warm breeze for early March pushed at them, but even the elements seemed to know better than to touch Gabe. "But he would have killed them, anyway, for nothing more than the crime of mentioning Darci's name."

Killed. Them. Killed Gabe—and killed Evangeline.

The reality of it sliced through her, those horrible blind seconds when the world had started to slide, when Gabe had sworn and reached for her, holding out an arm to protect, even as he fought with the truck.

He was right. They could have been killed, and no one would have known it was really murder. If Gabe hadn't known how to compensate for the sudden loss of one tire. If he hadn't stayed calm under pressure. If his reflexes had been slow.

If he'd taken pills that morning.

"The tire was tampered with," she said.

Gabe squatted next to the shredded remains. "Without a doubt."

"Can you prove it?"

He twisted toward her, his mouth a hard, grim line. "That's the thing with tampering, darlin'. If you know what you're doing, there's never any proof."

Somehow she kept standing there—and she was pretty sure the sunlight leaking through the trees hid the slow drain of color from her face. After only a heartbeat Gabe twisted back toward the tire. But his words kept right on weaving through her....

That's the thing with tampering...

A shiny black BMW raced by, but Evangeline barely saw, barely moved.

If you know what you're doing, there's never any proof.

That's what she was afraid of—what she'd risked everything to prove. That Gabriel Fontenot knew *exactly* what he was doing. She forced her eyes from the road back to him, watched him push to his feet and stride to the passenger side of the truck, lean inside. Less than a minute later he came out with the spare.

He also had the bill from the diner.

"I'll get this changed and call Jack, let him know what's going on."

Somehow she nodded. Somehow she stepped back as he passed and made herself look away from him, from the sweat gathering on his brow and the moisture seeping through the back of his shirt, toward the murky waters of the canal.

Behind her, Gabe muttered under his breath as he changed the tire. She'd known that he'd grown up in a rural community southwest of New Orleans, but she'd never imagined him this way, hot and sweaty and working on a car.

But as much as the image intrigued, as much as part of her wondered what part of Russell Rae was really Gabriel Fontenot, one word kept drilling through her.

Tampering.

Frowning, she wiped the moisture from her face and made her way back to the open door.

"Get me a water," Gabe called.

With a pretend smile she retrieved the bottle from the front seat and tossed it to him.

She didn't let herself linger on the smile he gave her in return. Reaching for her phone, she checked to make sure she had coverage, then placed the call.

It took three times to get through—what few cell towers there were in this part of the state had been badly damaged by Katrina. Some of them—a few of them—had been repaired. Most had not.

The soft voice answered on the first ring. "Dot's Bakery."

Evangeline squinted against the sun cutting through a tangle of Spanish moss. "I must have the wrong number, I was trying to reach—"

"You the gal from Rosemunde's?"

She stilled. "Yes."

Silence. For a long, thick heartbeat. "She said…" The girl—she had to be a girl—lowered her voice. "She said you were a friend of Darci's."

"Yes."

"So was I."

Live oaks lined the dirt road, their tattered canopies creating a tunnel leading to the faded white house at the end of the drive. Whispering Oaks sat there, big and grand and weathered, out of place and time but still beautiful.

"I've heard about this place," Evangeline said as Gabe swerved the pickup toward a wooded area beyond the oak-shrouded drive. There was no sign of the girl they'd arranged to meet. "Didn't they make a movie here?"

"A couple of them," he said. "But it's been a while."

Once the plantation had been the heart of the parish. Even decades after she'd fallen into disrepair, tourists had found their way here. If Evangeline remembered right, there'd been an attempt to turn the house into a bed-and-breakfast, but purists had balked at having even one shutter tampered with.

Tampered.

The word scraped, even as part of her wished this time the tampering had been allowed. Now in disrepair, Whispering Oaks, with her stunning rows of columns and wraparound porches, sat secluded by the trees, all but forgotten.

Much like Jimmy.

Except she hadn't forgotten, and even if her brother refused her visits, he wasn't alone. Four months had passed since she'd last driven away from the Louisiana State Penitentiary in Angola, but the vow she'd made that fall day remained like steel inside of her. She was getting close. No matter what went down with the girl who'd arranged to meet them here, Evangeline had other leads, starting with juror number eight. She'd tracked him down, and he was willing to talk.

In four days they would meet.

The quick slice of dread was automatic, the memory of juror number three, a young single mother from Chalmette who'd arranged to meet with Evangeline at a bowling alley. She'd been nervous, but ready to talk.

That had been almost a year before. Evangeline had sat there listening to the echo of bowling balls for six hours, but the woman had never shown. The next morning she'd read about the single-car accident. Cherry had been drinking and lost control…

In her small frame house, the police had found a shoe box containing newspaper clippings from the trial…and several other cases Gabe had prosecuted. No one had thought much about it. Cherry was, after all, a single woman. And Gabe, a Robichaud, was probably as close to a rock star as she'd ever met.

But Evangeline knew there was a darker side….

Swallowing against the sickness, she glanced at him, at the hard lines of his face and the determination in his eyes, and waited for the surge of venom. But her throat tightened instead, and she found herself looking at hands she'd once imagined covered in Cherry's blood. Now she saw only the grease from changing the tire, the blunt-tipped fingers and the calluses. She remembered the way those hands had felt the night before against her face, when he'd inspected the gash at her forehead.

Dangerous, she reminded herself, in more ways than one. That's why she looked away from his hands, to the forsaken old house. It was easier that way. She could think more clearly, focus her thoughts where they needed to be, not on some ridiculous fantasy of a man who didn't exist.

Like juror number three, the girl on the phone had been scared. Her voice had grown lower, until Evangeline had barely been able to hear her over the wind.

It had taken some coaxing to convince her to meet them, but she'd let the girl choose the time and the place. Out of view, Gabe parked the truck and turned off the engine.

"I don't see her," he said. "You sure we can trust her?"

There were only a few things Evangeline was sure of—the girl who claimed to be a friend of Darci's was not one of them. Too much desperation had leaked through her voice. "Depends upon how badly she wants to know what she thinks we can tell her."

Trees stretched and sprawled around the car, their roots running above ground like a tangle of thick snakes while cypress knees jutted up everywhere, making it nearly impossible for grass to grow. But not the moss. It dripped and dangled around them, swaying to an unheard rhythm.

It could have been the twenty-first century, or the nineteenth century. Other than the truck, there was no giveaway—no other vehicles, no radios or MP3 players or cell phones. Just the grand old house a hundred yards away.

And secrets waiting to be found.

"It's beautiful," she said. The winter had been mild and the Deep South rarely obeyed Mother Nature's rules. Against the porch out-of-control rosebushes tangled with wild bougainvillea, both in near-violent bloom—much like the bright pink-and-white flowers her mother had once tended to. "Like stepping back in time."

"That's what my sister always said."

His voice, quiet and oddly thick, rushed through Evangeline, because, for a fractured minute, she'd actually forgotten: forgotten why she'd come to New Orleans, forgotten that years had passed since her mother had tended to anything, forgotten she was there to pump an informant for information. Forgotten that Jimmy was in prison and juror number three was dead.

That Gabe was at the old house with her.

But even as she remembered, his voice buffered the broken edges she'd lived with for too long.

"I didn't know you had a sister," she said, and the image came by itself, that of a brother and a sister. Gabe would have been protective but annoying, just as Jimmy had been. He'd gone out of his way to drive her crazy, had put toads in her bed and given her favorite Barbie dolls crew cuts. But if anyone had laid a hand on her, or so much as looked at her the wrong way...

Jimmy had put a quick end to that.

And then someone had tampered with everything... and put an end to life as he'd known it.

"Camille," Gabe said, staring at the tired old house as if he expected someone to come running out any minute.

"Older or younger?" she asked. "Does she still live in Louisiana? I bet—" The memory clicked even though he said nothing, the black-and-white photo on the corner of his desk, the girl with the impish smile and blond hair. The picture had to be twenty years old. If that was his sister...

If he had a more recent picture...

Gabe loved his sister enough to keep a picture of her where he could see it often, but he'd never mentioned one word about Camille, not even before, during those first few weeks, when no walls had existed between them.

"Gabe." This time Evangeline's voice was quiet. And this time she did what she knew better than doing: she lifted her hand to his shoulder. "Did something happen to her?"

Beneath her hand, his muscles bunched, but he didn't turn to look at her. "I don't know."

It was not the answer she'd expected. "I don't understand."

"No one does." The words were quiet, clipped, not

at all like those of the exalted assistant district attorney or the good ole boy Russell Rae, but a man who didn't know how to let go. "Sometimes I still think I'm going to see her on the porch with a book or a magazine…."

"But you're not going to, are you?" The question was quiet, gentle.

"No."

She absorbed the word, felt the sense of loss down to her bone. "What happened?" she asked, but knew he didn't hear. Because he smiled. It was a slow smile, an easy curving of his lips.

"She used to say she'd lived here before," he said in that same restrained voice, while Evangeline wondered how it was possible that a smile could take years off his face—and his heart. "Back when the house was new—and that, someday, she'd live in it again."

There was so much to grab on to, so many questions to ask. In the end, she chose the most obvious. "You lived around here?"

Her research had focused on Gabriel Fontenot, the Robichaud and the attorney, the man. But not the boy.

"Other side of the parish," he said, and the surprise was immediate, not because of his answer, but because he *did* answer. Gabe did. He answered her question. *Hers.* Evangeline's. The woman who'd offered him friendship and compassion, while she'd been setting him up, praying he would fall.

"And you came here today, anyway?" The gamble surprised her. "What if someone recognized you?"

He shot her a look so dry, so classic Gabriel Fontenot, it was all she could do not to laugh. "Do *you* recognize me?"

This time she did laugh, even as something inside her

wanted to cry. "I'm not sure I ever knew you to begin with," she answered with an honesty that made her chest tighten. There was Gabe, the son of privilege, and Gabe, the cut-throat attorney; Gabe, the card shark, and Gabe, the coffee addict, Gabe, the man who'd been betrayed first by a colleague, then by the woman he was going to marry.

Gabe, who slipped easily into the role of Russell Rae.

Gabe, the brother, who had a picture of his sister on his desk.

Gabe, the vigilante.

"I stopped looking in the mirror," he said, not looking at her, either. "Until a few days ago."

Because even he didn't recognize the man he'd become. The words were unspoken, but they sliced through Evangeline, anyway.

"I've been gone a long time," he was saying, and suddenly she knew they'd traveled further back, to when he'd been a boy and his sister a girl, when he'd known where she was and what he would see in the mirror. "A lot's changed since then. No one in Wild Berry would ever guess."

Guess what? she wanted to ask. How far he'd risen, or how far he'd fallen?

"What happened?" Maybe she shouldn't have asked the question. She'd told herself not to let things get personal again. Not to ask questions, not to look beyond the facts as they pertained to her brother's case. But nothing happened in isolation. The fragmented man Gabe had become and the boy he'd been…they were both part of the puzzle. "To your sister?"

To him.

He looked beyond the old house, toward the bayou snaking along a couple hundred yards from the structure. "She was just a kid," he said. "Cute, sweet, with a big heart and an even bigger taste for adventure. She and Saura… No matter how many times I told them all those stories about religious relics smuggled out of France were just that, stories, they kept looking. They were so determined to be the ones to find it…just like my dad."

The smile just sort of happened. "I was a buried-treasure girl, myself," she said, and with the words came the memory. Of her and Jimmy and a silly Civil War treasure map purchased at a country grocery. "I was convinced if we looked hard enough, we'd find a stash of jewelry buried by some poor antebellum woman before her home was invaded." She'd heard the stories and rumors, of the women who'd buried their valuables in the swamp to prevent the Yankees from stealing them. According to her grandmother, her great-aunt had actually dug up a sterling-silver tea service for twelve. "Maybe even the lost Confederate gold."

That had been Jimmy's goal.

She stilled, realized she'd just handed Gabe a piece of herself, of Jimmy, she'd never meant to share.

But he didn't even act as if he'd heard. His hands were tight on the steering wheel now, his knuckles white. "She never knew when to stop. Never knew when to listen. Christ," he swore, and with the words, slammed one fist against the wheel. "If she'd just listened—"

Evangeline looked to the hard lines of his face. "If she'd just listened, what?"

Chapter 5

Four years separated them. By all rights, Gabe should have found Camille annoying. She'd left her dolls in his bed and taped lace curtains up in the fort he and Jack had constructed in the backyard. But every night before bed she'd told him she loved him, and every morning she'd offered to comb his hair.

That's what he wanted to remember, what he tried to remember.

Instead, when he thought of his sister, he saw eyes dark and damp and horrified, a pale mouth and tangled hair, clothes that were torn. He saw Jack running and her limp in his arms, alive, but…gone.

"It was late." Up ahead, darkness bled from the grimy windows, making it impossible to see what lay inside. "She should have been in bed, but she wanted to listen to records with me and Jack, kept offering to fix milk shakes or popcorn…" She'd been wearing one of their father's LSU football T-shirts. It had been huge on her, hanging like a dress.

"Gabe?"

Beside him he saw Evangeline move, was aware of her hand settling against his wrist. But he felt nothing. He turned anyway, looked at her angled toward him, compassion in her eyes.

It was a hell of an illusion.

He should have learned, damn it. That night, and in the days that followed. He should have learned that just because he wanted something to be one way, didn't mean that it was. "She told me she was going to bed."

Lilah— He destroyed the name before it could finish forming. Lilah didn't exist. It was Evangeline whose ponytail was loosening, Evangeline who looked at him with an understanding he knew better than to trust.

"But she didn't," she whispered.

"No, she didn't." He could still hear the song that had been playing when his mother's scream ripped through the last seconds of his childhood. It had been a debut album, a new rock band from Ireland. "She—" The memory hacked through all the debris he'd shoved against it. "She went somewhere she shouldn't have gone, saw something she shouldn't have seen."

"What?" Evangeline's hand tightened against his wrist. "What did she see?"

He tried to focus on her, but saw only a wood-paneled study lit by a single lamp. "The gun." His voice was so devoid of emotion he barely recognized it. "The blood." Everywhere. "The body."

Evangeline winced. "Your sister saw someone killed?" It was barely more than a whisper.

The door had been open, the cool breeze swirling through the room, giving the illusion of life to death. "She ran." He and Jack had found her footprints in the mud beyond their old fort. Hers, and another set. Larger.

"My God... Did the killer see her? Did he know what she'd seen?"

A hard sound broke from Gabe's throat. "Depends upon whose story you believe."

"Did you..." Wide and dark and drenched with something that made Gabe's chest tighten, Evangeline's eyes met his. "How long was she missing?"

Because he wanted so goddamn bad to touch, he ripped back and stared at the dials on the dashboard. "She didn't want to be found." Just like now. "We all looked, Uncle Eddy and Uncle Eti, Cain, Saura, me..."

But not his father.

"Jack found her two days later."

"Jack?" Recognition hovered on the name. "The sheriff you told me about? Savoie?"

They'd split up, Gabe going left, Jack going right. By then over fifty people had methodically combed the swamp. There'd been dogs. And so much unsaid. With each hour that passed, the quiet had thickened, the grim awareness hardening his uncles' eyes.

Shortly after sunrise Jack's shouts had brought them running. He'd emerged from a tangle of wild bougainvillea, his clothes wet and dirty and torn, Cami in his arms.

"He's like a brother to me," he said. "And to her."

Evangeline closed her eyes, opened them a long moment later. But the horror remained. "I'm so sorry, I know what it's like to—"

The words broke off, dangling there between them. "To what?" Gabe asked.

He saw her throat work. "It never goes away, does it?" With a sad smile, she shoved the flyaway hairs back from her face. "You remember the way things used to be, the plans and dreams for the future. But you're in that future now, and nothing is the way it's supposed to be. There's this big empty place that never goes away...."

Outside the truck, the wind kept blowing. And in the trees, the birds were squawking. Blackbirds, he thought. The herons that nested nearby were quiet. But Gabe didn't allow himself to move. Because if he did, it would be toward her. He would lift his hand and touch her cheek, see if she could possibly feel as good as he remembered.

If she needed his touch anywhere near as badly as he needed—

"Come on. Let's go." He reached for the door and pushed it open, stepped into the warm breeze. He hadn't brought Evangeline here to trade secrets or play true confessions, damn it. "She should be here by now," he practically growled the words, striding toward the house.

From behind him he heard the other truck door close, Evangeline hurry after him. *"Gabe!"* she called, catching up with him on the sweeping wraparound porch. "What are you so afraid of?"

He spun toward her, found her too damn close. He couldn't move without touching her, couldn't breathe without inhaling the scent of powder and vanilla. "Law 101," he said silkily. They were attorneys. They both knew how to sidestep. "Never ask a question unless you really want the answer."

Her smile was slow, languorous. "Law 201," she countered. "When you don't want to answer a question, fire another one in return."

Slowly, he lifted his hands. And slowly they came

down on her arms. That's when she should have winced. That's when she should have recoiled, twisted from his arms and backed away. Because she knew, damn it. She knew she'd betrayed him. She knew she'd peppered him with lies to see if he would bite. She knew, and she knew that he knew.

But she made no move to get away from him, just angled her chin and looked up at him in much the way she looked at a witness she was on the verge of cracking.

The urge to move his hands higher slayed him. To slide a finger along her jawbone and free the hair from her mouth, to put the pads of his fingers there, to trace and touch and—

Taste.

Because *he* knew, too. He remembered. Her taste and her feel, the confidence and uncertainty. But he also knew how easily she could morph like a chameleon into whatever she needed to get what she wanted.

"This isn't a game," he said very quietly, but as her eyes flared, the lie echoed like a shout. It *was* a game. He was with her for one reason and one reason only: to nail Marcel Lambert. When the bastard was behind bars, this pretend alliance would fall away, leaving only the residue of lies.

"Five minutes," he said, pivoting toward the door. "And then I'm outta here."

The sound came first, that of shuffling from the windows toward the right. Then the voice, soft and young. Nervous. *"D-don't go."*

He reached for the doorknob, but before he could turn it, Evangeline put her hand to his. *"No."* Her voice was soft, her touch forceful. "You'll scare her."

He stilled at the words, hated that she was right.

"Let me," she said, and when he twisted back to her, when he saw the calm warmth that had once been his hallmark glowing in her eyes, he knew if anyone could coax the girl into talking, it was Evangeline.

But he didn't release her hand. He curled his fingers with hers and led her toward the grimy windows.

"Don't be afraid." She spoke to the girl, but her eyes met Gabe's. "We'll play this by your rules."

Motioning for Evangeline to step closer, he made himself wait two steps behind.

"Y'all aren't the first, you know," the girl said, and Evangeline stopped abruptly, shooting a quick glance at Gabe. He nodded, gestured for her to ask the question.

"Not the first to what?"

Beyond her, the first traces of an afternoon thunderstorm darkened the horizon. With it the breeze rushed through the old columns, rattling the panes of the window. "To come here," the girl said. "Ask questions about Darci."

Gabe tensed.

"Is that why you're scared?" Evangeline stood just outside the window now. "Is that why you wanted to meet here and not in the city?"

"Rosemunde says they're still here, even if I can't see them. That they're watching."

The way they watched Gabe. Silently. From the shadows. He felt them, even if he hadn't seen them. They were getting bolder. Last night they'd tipped off Evangeline. Today they'd blown out his tire.

"Who?" Evangeline asked. "Who's here?"

"The men," the girl said, and her voice shook. "The ones who know who killed Darci."

And who wanted to make damn sure no one stepped forward to strengthen the prosecution's case.

Gabe stepped closer, but Evangeline held up her arm and shook her head. "What do they want?"

A shadow shifted. "They came to the bakery, asking questions and showing pictures, said it was too bad about Darci, that it sure would be a shame if she wasn't the only one to meet her maker earlier than expected."

The words ground through Gabe. He stepped to Evangeline and put his hand to the small of her back. "That's not going to happen," he vowed with a roughness his poker buddies wouldn't have believed possible, not from cool, calm, always-in-control, Fontenot.

"I'm not—" He broke off, remembered he was supposed to be Russell Rae the friend of Darci's, not Gabe the avenger. "Sheriff Savoie won't let that happen."

"Did…did she seem scared to you? The last time I talked to her, she seemed so happy…."

The sadness in the girl's voice got to him. She'd been Darci's friend. She'd loved her. The thought of those final moments, when Darci had clawed against the hands wrapped around her throat…

Gabe knew what those thoughts did to a person.

"Things spun out of control fast," he said, and the gentleness came easily. Saura had seen Darci at a party a few days before her death. Wide-eyed, she'd said. Skittish.

"I don't think she knew she was in danger," Evangeline added, but they both knew that was a lie. Darci had called D'Ambrosia the morning of her death.

"Not until the very end," Evangeline added.

"Did she say anything to you?" Gabe asked. "About *him?*"

Above the increasing caw of the birds, he heard the girl's sharp intake of breath. *"Marcel?"* Gabe could practically see her making the sign of the cross—not in fear, but adoration. "He didn't do it. He couldn't have."

"How do you know that?" Evangeline's voice was calm and reassuring, the way it always was when she cross-examined and bluffed.

"I—I saw them together," Darci's friend stammered. "He looked at her the way every girl wants to be looked at. And he promised…"

Gabe leaned closer. They'd gotten to her, the men at the country grocery or someone else on Lambert's payroll. They'd compromised her. This was all some kind of clever setup or game, just like the meet the night before— "Promised what?"

"To take care of her," she said softly, and inside the house, the shadows deepened, making it impossible to discern where she stood. "That's why he…"

Marcel had taken care of Darci, all right. "Why he what?" Gabe asked.

Silence.

He narrowed his eyes, felt his heart slam. "Why he *what?*" But even as the words ripped from him, he knew there would be no answer.

"She's gone," Evangeline said.

"Like hell." Gabe ran to the front door, put his hand to the knob and kicked it open. Inside, the tired old house groaned around him, the curved stairway to the right and the wide hall running through the center, the twin parlors on either side. "Why he *what?*" he shouted again.

She'd slipped. She'd almost told them something. He took off through the shadows toward the back of the house, through the ballroom to the dining room, where a single door flapped in the breeze. *"Why he what?"*

"Gabe."

It was only his name; that was all she said. But the sound of it on her voice, all soft and sincere and...concerned, slipped through him like a slow slide of whiskey. He rejected the surge, didn't let himself move when he felt her touch. She came up from behind him and put her hands to his back, as if she had every goddamn right to do so. Then she pressed her body to his, gentle, intimate. As if they were in this together.

"She's gone."

And for a jagged white moment, he didn't know who the hell she meant—Darci's friend, or the cutthroat attorney who'd lifted her mouth to his, even as she'd driven the knife into his back.

"He got to her." His throat burned on the words. He stared beyond the back porch, where the sprawl of oaks sloped down to the lazy bayou. "She's scared out of her mind."

"She is," Evangeline agreed, and the words feathered against the side of his neck. "But that doesn't mean she's lying."

He turned to her without thinking, raised his hands before he could make himself stop. Still he didn't touch, didn't let himself. But he could do nothing about what he saw in her eyes, the dark, dark swirl. The uncertainty.

The need.

"Maybe she's just confused," she said as the breeze blew a few strands of hair against her mouth. "Maybe she's just trying to make sense out of what happened."

"Then she's a fool," he said, stripping every shred of emotion from his voice. That had been his hallmark, his trademark. No emotion, strip it all away. Say what had to be said, do what had to be done, then walk away from the carnage, move on, don't look back.

Even if something dangerously close to hurt flashed in Evangeline's eyes.

"Let's go." He closed the door and headed toward the front of the house. "There's nothing here."

"I'm not so sure about that."

He should have kept walking. He should have kept straight on for the truck and gotten inside, not looked back. But the note of discovery made him turn.

She stood where he'd left her, by the back door with her flyaway shirt blowing in the breeze, hair still stuck against her lips. But in her hand she held a business card.

"Dot's Bakery," she said, flipping it over. Her eyes met his, a slow smile curved her lips. "It's a map."

On the outside it looked like an old hunting cabin. The wood was weathered, the foliage overgrown. Vines climbed the front. Ferns sprang up around the foundation. A few simple white flowers bloomed foolishly. And the live oaks sprawled in all directions. It was like stepping into a still life.

Evangeline let Gabe approach first, knowing that it was somehow important. He'd spoken little since they'd left the plantation. For the most part he'd kept a hand on the wheel and his eyes on the road. Taking the three steps leading to the Acadian-style porch, he strode toward the door. But then he stopped and turned toward an artful arrangement of clay pots. Seven of them, four different sizes. They all contained dead plants. Annuals, she would guess from the weathered stems. Pansies.

Their gazes collided, and the shock curled clear down to her toes. He was a man of Armani suits, leather briefcases and Italian shoes, but somehow the low-riding blue jeans and grease-stained ivory button-down looked…right. And for a fractured moment, she could almost see him pulling a hose to the pots and watering the flowers.

The image jarred her. She'd prepared relentlessly, had forced herself to plan through every scenario—to confront Gabe, to battle him. To bring him down.

But, God help her, it had never occurred to her that she would like him. *Want* him. It shouldn't have been possible, not with Jimmy rotting in Angola and juror number three's daughter being raised by a shattered grandmother.

But there it was, there it had been from the start. When he looked at her, her throat tightened. In disgust, she'd told herself. Contempt. Maybe even anticipation. For making sure he paid for his sins, she wanted to believe, but not this, not seeing him on an old weathered porch in the middle of nowhere, watering plants.

It was too simple, too…innocent.

Shoving the unwanted image aside, she joined him on the wide porch and went for the door, stopped at the welcome mat. Not old and faded like everything else, but bright and cheery and…new.

Then she put her hand to the knob and turned, stepped inside and stopped.

The more the pieces fell together, the more they refused to fit.

Then Gabe was there, standing a step too close. "What the hell—"

As her eyes adjusted to the hazy light, she took it all in, the white lace curtains and the pink-and-cream braided rugs, the quaint arrangement of furniture and the state-of-the-art electronics. The photograph. "Darci…"

And Marcel.

In a small old-fashioned frame, the picture sat on a wicker table next to a cream sofa in a pattern of peach and buttery yellow hydrangeas. His arm was around her. She was leaning into him. They were both smiling.

Evangeline moved toward it, knew better than to touch it. Going down on a knee, she studied the image, looking for something dark or sinister lurking beneath the surface.

Gabe kept going, taking long hard strides toward the closed door at the back of the room. Using his shirttail, he put his hand to the knob and pushed inside.

Beyond him she could see the bed, big and brass with a white lace canopy draped over the top. Joining him, she took in the rest of the small room, the pine dresser with a vase of dead flowers on top, the wood trunk at the foot of the bed, the bookcase filled with paperbacks and more framed photographs—all of Darci and Marcel.

Gabe swore softly. "Well, isn't this cozy?"

"This wasn't in the police report," Evangeline said. There'd been no mention of a cabin on the outskirts of Wild Berry, belonging to Darci or Marcel. He was a married man. He had a house on the lake in the city, a summer home that had been destroyed by Katrina near Pass Christian, Mississippi. A condo in Aspen. Both had been searched. Nothing linking the restaurateur to an inappropriate relationship with a woman young enough to be his daughter had been found.

But this…

Anticipation quickened through Evangeline—the evidence here would keep the investigative team busy for days. "We need to call D'Ambrosia," she said, reaching into her purse for her phone.

Gabe's hand to her wrist stopped her. "Not yet."

She twisted toward him, saw the hard look in his eyes,

and before he even took the first step, she knew that he had no intention of waiting for anyone else. He broke from her and crossed to the dresser, stabbed his hand into the wrinkled fabric of his shirt. Then he yanked open a drawer. And another. From inside the third he pulled out two pillowcases—peach in a rose chintz pattern—and tossed one to her. "You want the bedroom or the front room?"

The television alone would set someone back at least three grand. No way had Darci furnished the cabin on her own—if she'd ever even been here to begin with.

The stack of CDs seemed right, though, a collection of pop and country, with two popular new-age bands thrown in. And the celebrity-gossip magazines made sense. The latest Cameron Monroe book, *Secret Sins,* struck him as ironic.

In the kitchen he found two boxes of green tea, one with five tea bags missing, pomegranate juice in the re-frigerator next to a pricey bottle of white wine and a six-pack of beer, none missing. The cheese was molded, the sandwich meat reeked. But there was no milk, nothing with a date that would indicate how long the cabin had stood empty.

"Gabe."

He turned to find Evangeline standing in the doorway to the bedroom. With late afternoon, the light filtering through the windows had faded, leaving shadows to spill around her.

"You need to see this," she said, and the stillness deepened, not gently as it had before, but with a hard, jagged slice straight through him.

She was wrong. He didn't need to see this, didn't

want to see this, her standing in the doorway to a bed-room, looking soft and sweet and goddamned innocent, with wisps of cinnamon hair spilling around her face and anticipation glowing in her eyes.

But he closed the refrigerator and moved toward her, followed when she led him to a chest at the foot of the bed and went down on her knees. Envelopes lay scattered across the floor, two notebooks, a collection of poems by Elizabeth Barrett Browning.

"You're not going to like this," she said, using the pillowcase to hand him a stack of what looked to be letters.

He took them from her, careful to keep the chintz between his hand and the paper. The sound of the anxious birds beyond the window faded as he looked down at the first, taking in the bold, masculine handwriting—and the soft, love-struck words.

> …like sunshine in my otherwise dreary life…
> …take you away from all this, from here, the pain and the memories, to keep you safe, keep you mine…

He slapped the page aside and looked at another, and another.

> …when you touch me, my world stands still…
> …your smile gives my life meaning…

He glanced up and found Evangeline watching him, and knew her thoughts mirrored his. "A jury will eat this stuff up," she said.

A hard sound broke from his throat. "If they don't throw up, first."

Her smile was soft, sad. "Keep going, there's more."

He did as she said and soon found the second hand-writing, softer and prettier, but juvenile somehow; the letters large and carefully formed, the ink pink.

…don't know what I'd do without you…

And all Gabe could think was, *how damn convenient.*

"It doesn't make sense," Evangeline said, swiping the flyaway hairs from her face. "For the defense, this stuff is golden. So why hasn't it been found before now? Why didn't Lambert's team lead the cops here?"

Gabe dropped the letters and reached for the note-book. "Cover-ups take time."

"Cover-ups?"

"We're here now for a reason," he said. "Someone wants us here." Just as someone had wanted Evangeline at the warehouse the night before. "Someone wants *us* to find this stuff."

"You think Lambert—"

"I *know* Lambert." He just wasn't sure why, yet. Or how all the pieces fit. "He's smooth. He's good. There's no way he would just sit on evidence like this…."

"He's denied having the affair," Evangeline pointed out. That was a big part of why they'd come to Wild Berry in the first place, to find evidence of the relationship.

"This," she said, gesturing to the notebook in his hands, the gooey, high school-esque poetry written in a man's hand, "blows the lid off that."

"Maybe that's what he wants." Lambert's claim that he and Darci were just friends was unraveling. The cops had a witness who'd seen them together. Allegedly even a photograph. The longer he clung to the lie, the more suspicion fell his way.

"You think he's filling in the blanks," Evangeline said, "before the jury does it for him."

He flipped another page, tried not to laugh:

Vaster than the stars and deeper than the oceans…

Lambert knew he couldn't keep his relationship with Darci a secret. This way, with the prosecution uncovering evidence that showed how much he loved her, he could shape the jury's perceptions, himself, rather than allowing them to come to their own perverted conclusions. "Marcel Lambert, lovesick victim," he muttered.

"Or hero." The words were quiet.

He looked up and found her extending a single sheet of paper toward him. He took it, stared down at the more scrawled, but still juvenile, handwriting:

He won't leave me alone. I told him we're over, but he won't accept no for an answer. Help me, Marci. Tell me how to make him leave me alone—

"Son of a bitch." Gabe practically growled. "He's good."

"What if he's innocent?" Evangeline asked, and the question twisted through him. It was the same one she'd asked the day before. "What if this is real?"

"It's not." Dropping the letter, he stood and strode to the window, where streaks of red swirled against a pale blue sky.

Reflected in the glass, he saw Evangeline move, saw her come to her feet and step toward him. He didn't move, just watched her destroy the distance between them and tried not to drown on the scent of powder and vanilla.

She touched him, settled her hands on his biceps slowly, tentatively, as if there were a chance the cotton of his shirt might scald her hands.

"Gabe." Through the reflection, her eyes met his. "It was Marcel, wasn't it?"

It shouldn't have been possible for everything around him to tilt and spin like an out-of-control carnival ride, when everything inside of him just stopped.

"It was him, wasn't it?" she said. "That's why you can't let this case go…why you're so sure Marcel Lambert is guilty—your sister saw him kill your father."

Chapter 6

The answer glowed in Gabe's eyes.

Evangeline told herself to look away, turn away, but standing behind him, with dusk falling around them and the shadows deepening, she could no more move than she could breathe.

It hurt to look at him. It hurt to see. But through the hazy reflection, the truth came into focus. She'd realized Gabe had an unnatural fixation on Marcel Lambert. She'd known he had a vendetta, that his desire to nail the restaurateur vibrated with an intensity that belied objectivity. At first she'd thought it was just his desire to get back in the saddle and win, to sink his teeth into something and come out on top.

Watching his eyes, fixed on some point in the distance, she knew he did not see the skeletal cypress or the tangle of oaks, the leaves swirling with the breeze.

Because it was not a man's eyes she saw, but a boy's…
A boy whose world had shattered.

From the very first she'd been fascinated with him,
Gabe, the man, the brash young attorney working his
very first case, even though he'd been leading the prosecution against her brother. There'd been a sincerity
to him, a charisma that had enchanted the bright-eyed
eighteen-year-old she'd been. His gaze had met hers during the opening arguments, and she would have sworn
she saw a flicker of compassion, maybe even commis-
eration, and for a fleeting heartbeat, hope had trickled
through her.

But then the case had begun, and the ambitious
Southern attorney had gotten to work. Within weeks her
brother's future had been snatched away, despite the
flimsy evidence. And her mother had started to drink.
To sit on the front porch and rock, insisting her baby had
been framed. That Gabriel Fontenot had been unable to
secure a conviction on his first case the honest way, so
he'd secured it the old-fashioned way, with cold, hard
Robichaud cash.

The allegations had seemed ludicrous at first, the
result of too much bourbon and sorrow. But then
Evangeline's favorite teacher had echoed the specula-
tion, as had her best friend's father, and she'd started to
wonder.

To hate.

But it wasn't hate that ripped through her now,
wasn't all those hard, destructive edges she'd used to
shape her life.

"Tell me," she said, even though she knew it was dangerous to allow herself to see Gabe this way, to know
the boy who'd lost his childhood. *"Please."*

The shadows on his face deepened. "No one believed her—not even me."

Somehow she kept herself from curving her arms around his middle and holding on, from laying her head against his back. But she could do nothing about the longing, the insane wish that they were two different people, in a different time and place, without a reservoir of lies and doubt festering between them.

"It didn't make sense," he said in the same detached monotone witnesses used to recount something horrific. "No one even knew they were friends."

She didn't let herself move, knew better than to take that last step toward him.

"She didn't talk for two days. The doctors said it was shock, the trauma of seeing Dad blow his brains out."

Evangeline closed her eyes, didn't want to see.

"She just sat there in that hospital bed and stared straight ahead. We took turns staying with her, my mother and my uncles, Cain and Saura and Jack—"

"I can't even imagine," she whispered, and though she did not want to see, she willed her eyes to open.

"Jack was with her when she started talking. I was coming back with coffee and I heard her scream, started to run. I found him holding her, trying to soothe her, quiet her. But she just kept screaming."

And Evangeline couldn't do it any longer, couldn't just stand there when she knew that Gabe saw it all over again—his sister in his best friend's arms, incoherent and screaming. Not when the need to hold on sliced clear to the bone. She slid her arms around his waist and pressed closer, rested her head against his back. "I'm so sorry…"

"She saw him." With those words the grief of the boy

hardened into the vengeance of the man. "She saw him shot dead…but no one believed her."

Outside, the hard rush of the wind had stopped, dropping the leaves back to the ground as fat drops of rain splattered against the ground.

"They said it was self-inflicted, that there was no evidence of anyone else being in the room. That the horror of what Cami had seen was too great for her young mind to process, so she'd changed it, invented a shooter to take the blame off her daddy…."

It wasn't all that uncommon. Human nature demanded someone to blame, to punish…

"And she just…retreated, faded almost. She was scared to sleep alone. For almost a year she'd slept with my mother or in my bottom bunk. But she never screamed again, never mentioned that night—until she saw Marcel Lambert on the news."

Evangeline lifted her head from his back. And in the window's glass, their gazes met again. "What happened?"

Gabe's eyes were dark, shadowed. "She knew. The second she saw him, heard his voice…"

The image formed by itself, a young girl watching television—and coming face-to-face with her father's killer.

"It was him," Gabe said, and in her arms, she felt his body tense. "But there wasn't one shred of evidence."

So the man had gone on to live his life, to achieve fame as a celebrated restaurateur and chef, while two children had been left to grow up without a father. "Gabe—"

He twisted toward her, looked at her through eyes hard and dark and…tortured. But something else glittered in the cobalt, something raw and exposed, as if he'd just realized who he'd been talking to…or that he'd been talking, at all.

And then the moment shattered and he was jerking his cell phone from his pocket and stabbing a series of numbers.

The quick stab of rejection stunned her. Because of her brother, she told herself. She needed to get close to Gabe to find the evidence that would prove he'd secured a wrongful conviction of Jimmy. She'd already combed Gabe's files and records at the courthouse. Now she needed access to his house—his memories.

It would be far easier to obtain that access as his friend, his confidante, than his enemy.

"You need to see this," he said, without wasting time on greeting or explanation. Then he barked out directions. "I'm not going anywhere," he said, then snapped the phone shut and shoved it back into his pocket.

"D'Ambrosia?" His cousin's fiancé, the one who'd found Darci's body, had been instrumental in the investigation.

"Jack." Without another word, he went back to the chest, squatted and continued to sift through its contents. But she stood there for a long moment afterward, hating the way he could push her away, wall her out, without so much as lifting a hand. He'd slipped, she knew. He'd told her more than he wanted to, more than he'd intended to. For a few tenuous moments, he'd looked at her the way he had before, with a warm light in his eyes.

Quiet spilled between them as she joined him at the foot of the bed. Outside the rain came down in sheets, with no wind or lightning or thunder, just a soft patter against the windows. She wouldn't call it a storm, only a shower, and knew that soon enough the cloudburst would pass.

In Louisiana, they almost always did.

But this wouldn't, she thought, watching Gabe thumb through a stack of photographs. He'd slipped the pillowcase back around his hand, preserving evidence that was a significant blow to the prosecution's case against Marcel Lambert. A jury—*any jury*—would have a hard time believing a man could write such poetic and heartfelt words to a woman one week and strangle her to death the next.

Except Evangeline knew juries could be persuaded through other means….

Gabe could have destroyed it, she realized abruptly. Gabe could have boxed up every damning letter, every poem and photograph, and dumped them into the swamp, where no one would have found it.

Instead, he'd called his childhood friend, the local sheriff.

The realization did cruel, cruel things to the image of this man she'd carried in her heart for twelve years. "If someone wanted us to find this," she said, "that means they know Russell Rae and Lilah don't really exist."

A small wallet-sized photo in his hand, he looked up. "And that surprises you?"

No. Not really. Marcel Lambert was an influential man. Whether or not he was guilty of murder, he was more than capable of manipulation. "Those men at the country grocery. You think—"

Gabe's eyes hardened, and even though he said nothing, she had her answer. And the insidious irony of it sickened—what better way to plant evidence, than to have the prosecution be the ones to find it?

Frowning, she picked up the second pillowcase and

helped him sort the letters and poems and photographs into piles. Some of them actually had dates.

She wasn't sure how much time had passed when Gabe's cell phone rang. She only knew that the rain had slowed and the sky had begun to lighten. It was a simple no-nonsense ring, and Gabe had the phone in his hands and to his face within seconds.

"Sweet mercy," he growled, and the rough edge to his voice cut right through her. "How bad?"

Through the distorted connection, sirens wailed. Gabe gripped the small phone and tried to hear, but could only make out random words. "Fire…" Jack shouted above the distortion, "…Pecan Street…be a while."

Gabe glanced at the stacks of letters and pictures, the pillowcase balled up around his hand. "Do what you need to do," he said. "I'm not going anywhere."

Swearing softly, he closed the phone and tossed it onto the floor, stared at a white edge protruding from the stack of photographs.

"What's wrong?"

The question sliced through him. For close to thirty minutes, there'd been nothing—because before that, there'd been too damn much. He was a man of great control. He knew when to hold and when to fold, how to keep his eyes flat and his mouth even flatter. He knew how to bluff and how to lead.

But like a goddamned fool, he'd told her about the night Camille saw Marcel Lambert murder his father.

And he'd almost turned. When Evangeline had touched him, when she'd curved her arms around his body and rested her head against his back, he'd almost turned and put his arms around her, held her…

Looking up, he watched her kneeling less than a foot away, her eyes dark and serious and...*concerned—goddamn it*—and felt the shock of discovery tighten through him like a piece of bombshell evidence that changed everything.

And for the first time in months, he allowed himself to see her as she'd been those first few weeks, when she'd given him soft smiles and wise counsel, when she'd been there for him after they thought Alec had died, when she'd touched him and—

When she'd touched him. Because, sweet Christ, have mercy, she had. Touched him.

"Gabe?" Her eyes went a little wider, with a sharp edge he didn't want to be fear, the way they had the night he'd stormed into her office and asked her to deny what his uncle had told him, that she, Evangeline, had been setting him up, to see if he would fall. "What's wrong?"

"You didn't have a choice, did you?"

She blinked. "What?"

"You didn't know me," he said, and the words, the truth, scraped on the way out. *Black-and-white,* she'd said when they were in the warehouse. *That's all you see, isn't it?* All he'd ever seen.

All that could be trusted.

So he shoved everything else aside, all those deceptive shades of gray, and focused on what he knew to be real. "There's a fire in Bayou d'Espere." In an old section of town where Jack's grandmother lived. "Jack's going to be a while."

Evangeline closed the journal she'd been flipping through. "That's odd. There wasn't any lightning."

"Could have been a candle," he said, noting again a

white edge sticking out from the neat stack of photos. "Someone smoking in bed." Or something more sinister. Odd things had been happening in Bayou d'Espere. Random break-ins, including at the historical society and city hall, but no one had found anything missing. The week before, Jack had mentioned a fire at a local storage building.

Frowning, Gabe reached for the picture jutting out from the pile and found it stuck to the back of a picture of Marcel. He pulled it free…and found Darci smiling up at him. She looked young. Couldn't have been more than seventeen or eighteen, he guessed. A soft light glowed in her eyes, a guilelessness he'd not seen in the other pictures. Her dress was long and soft and pink… Completely different than the more risqué outfits she'd sported in New Orleans.

"What's that?" Evangeline asked.

Next to Darci stood a tall young man in a white tuxedo with a pink bow and cummerbund. His dark brown hair was a little shaggy, his cheeks ruddy. Behind them, centered beneath a balloon arch, a sign read: Congratulations Seniors!

"A prom picture."

Evangeline scooted closer. "She looks so young."

And innocent. That's what got him, the simplicity of the picture—hell, he had one like it stashed somewhere in his mother's attic—a boy and girl ready to embark on life.

"How does it happen?" Evangeline's voice was quiet as she reached for the picture. "How does a girl go from this to a rich man's plaything in only a couple of months?"

"I've seen it before," Gabe said. Too damn many times to count. "My first case…"

Crouched beside him, Evangeline twisted toward him. "Your first case, what?"

There was an odd rasp to her voice, as if she thought he was about to confess to something she did not want to hear. "Sometimes I can still see him." Tall and lanky, his hair cut with razor precision, his big body stuffed into a suit a size too small. "He had his whole damn life ahead of him."

Evangeline looked up from the prom photo and pierced him with eyes a little too narrow, a lot too dark. "What happened?"

"Quarterback of his high-school football team, short-stop on the baseball team, state title in track." Jimmy, his name had been. "Full scholarship to Louisiana State. His girlfriend was a cheerleader…" But he'd come to New Orleans for the summer, taken a job cleaning pools in an elite neighborhood.

Until one of his clients, the trophy wife of an investment banker, turned up strangled to death.

"I should have lost that case," Gabe muttered. He still did not understand how the jury had not seen even a shadow of doubt. The evidence had been circumstantial, at best.

Evangeline's mouth worked, but it was a moment before words formed. "What do you mean you should have lost? You didn't think he was guilty?"

Gabe looked down at the picture—but saw only Jimmy in handcuffs as he'd been led away. Gabe should have felt victory, triumph. "Juries are unpredictable." The smallest piece of evidence could sway them. They were coached to reach a verdict without emotion, to study fact and not possibility. So were lawyers. The last time he'd checked up on Jimmy—

He shoved the image, the gaunt man in the photo, from his mind. "We need a name," he said, studying the prom photo. Darci's date had not been interviewed by the police. If they could find him—

"Wow," Evangeline whispered, and then he saw what she saw, the five words scrawled on the back of the photo: *I'll love you forever.*

Frustration came hard and fast. It was a foolishly romantic vow, the kind of careless words that got spoken too damn often—and that attorneys could twist way too easily.

The pictures, the poems and letters, and now, Christ, a shaggy-haired boy who'd vowed to love Darci forever. Juries convicted and acquitted on a hell of a lot less.

"Gabe—" Evangeline started, but he was already on his feet and striding across the perfectly staged little room.

"It's not going to work," he vowed, stabbing his hand into the pillowcase and yanking open dresser drawers. Very little lay inside, a few changes of clothes, silk panties and a soft pink chemise, a bottle of sensuous massage oil. "This game—" he left the dresser and headed to the nightstand, ran his hand beneath the edge "—I'm not playing."

Evangeline came up behind him and put her hand to his, stopped his jerky movements. "Gabe—"

He spun on her before she could say anything else. "He's setting us up," he snapped, and felt the hot certainty clear down to his gut. "None of this is in the police report because none of this even existed four weeks ago." He would bet his life on it. "He brought you to me last night just like he brought us here today." The place was probably wired, Lambert listening—or even watching. And loving every second of it. "He wants us to find this, to—"

"Gabe." It was the third time she'd said only his name, but this time it was soft and gentle, and when he looked at her, when he looked down at her, the devastation in her eyes rocked him. "But you called Jack, anyway," she whispered. "You know what's in this house could sink the case against Lambert, but you didn't walk away, didn't pretend you hadn't seen anything. You cataloged every piece of information and called the sheriff…."

The confusion in her voice scraped through him. It almost sounded as if she'd expected him to suppress the evidence.

"What kind of man do you think I am?" he asked, but she didn't need to say a word to answer. Her slight wince said everything. Evangeline had no idea what kind of man he was, not anymore: the assistant district attorney who made mincemeat of witnesses, or the card shark who loved to bluff. The almost-lover who'd kissed her as though he never wanted to stop.

The man who'd condemned her without giving her a chance to explain.

The one who took pain pills or drank too much.

Or the Gabe who stood there now, in the shadows of twilight, looking down at the woman who'd fed him false information, but wanting to take her face into his hands, anyway, to put his mouth to hers and see if she still tasted like peppermint and innocence and—

Salvation.

The word should have made him turn away. Sweet mercy, it should have made him rip away.

But he lifted his hands to the sides of her face, feathering along the bruise at her cheekbone—the bruise he had put there. "You didn't know me," he murmured again, and this time his mouth lowered toward hers. In some distorted corner of his mind he heard her sharp intake of breath and knew he should pull back, but he could grab on to nothing except the longing flooding her eyes, the way her lips parted in a silent echo of his name.

Warmth swam through him the second his mouth took hers. She should have shoved him away. Instead, she stepped closer, moving into him, against him, and lifted her arms to curl around his neck. And held on tight.

Then her mouth was moving against his, his against hers, soft at first, gentle and sweet and tentative, giving way to a hard rush he'd tried so damn hard to destroy. It broke through him now, had him pulling her into his body. She moaned softly and threaded a hand through his hair, opened her mouth and let him in.

The dark swirl sucked harder, deeper, threatening to pull him under. But he didn't care, didn't fight the irrational greed, just slanted his mouth against hers and ran his hands along the soft lines of her body—the way he'd done before.

Before.

Before he'd analyzed anything too closely and before he'd fallen, when he'd just let himself feel. And want.

And damn near drown.

Chapter 7

The need rocked Evangeline. It was base and it was primal and it streaked through her on one powerful wave after another. In some barely functioning realm of her mind she knew she should pull away, shove at him with everything she had to put as much distance between them as she could, end this stupid charade. Russell Rae and Lilah didn't exist, couldn't exist.

It was Gabe kissing her, *Gabe!* But as his mouth moved against hers, everything blurred and there was only Gabe. He was a strong man. He prided himself on staying in control. But there was nothing controlled about the way his hands moved along her body—or the way her body responded. Heat swirled, making her knees go weak and overriding every sliver of caution or fear, leaving only a restless ache, the same ache that had shredded her the first time she'd realized she wanted a man she'd believed to be without conscience.

It was supposed to be black-and-white. For the first time in her life, it was supposed to be black-and-white….

But now the gray consumed her. His hands slid intimately along her body, along the curve of her waist and over the swell of her bottom, urging her closer and making it impossible not to feel the ridge pressed against her abdomen.

For over three months there'd been nothing. No touches, no smiles, no looks. And she'd told herself it was better that way. That she wouldn't lose focus. But beneath that facade the heat had smoldered, and now the truth of it washed through her—and shattered. She'd come to New Orleans to prove this man guilty of jury tampering—

She ripped out of his arms and staggered back. "No…"

Gabe stood there in the clothes of Russell Rae, his hair rumpled and his mouth swollen from the sheer greed of her kiss, but in the dark blue of his eyes glowed a horror that sliced clear down to the bone. "Evie…"

"No," she said again, and this time she moved, turned from him and practically ran from the room, the bed she'd wanted him to lay her down on. And feel him over her—inside her.

In the main room she headed straight for the front door and yanked it open, welcomed the slap of rain-cooled air like a touch of salvation she did not deserve.

Here the grayness fell gently, surrounding and swirling, bringing with it the mist and the sweet, misplaced scent of honeysuckle. She breathed it in, crossed to the rail and held on tight, closed her eyes and tilted her face toward the soft spray.

When she'd first come to New Orleans, everything had been so clear. Jimmy was in prison and her mother lost to alcohol, juror number three dead. The pieces had all been there; the opportunity she'd spent twelve years creating. Then she'd walked into that dinky little cafeteria and had seen Gabe staring at the charred remains inside a coffeepot. He'd turned to her and—

Banking the memory, she forced herself to go further back, to think of Jimmy, to remember *his* smile, his laugh. The life *he'd* dreamed about. He'd wanted to be a pediatrician. Her big bad jock of a brother had wanted to give his life to children....

"Evie."

Gabe's voice went through her, soft and warm and unbearably tender, just as his touch did. She stiffened, could feel him behind her. The heat of his body should have chased away the chill of the early-evening rain.

"Don't," she whispered. *"Please."*

For a moment, there was only the patter of the rain, the pounding of her heart. Then she heard him let out a hard breath as he removed his hand from her arm and stepped away.

"My grandparents lived in a house like this," she said without thinking. Her gaze remained fixed on the trees, the wind playing through the Spanish moss. "In the country, away from everything." With cats. Lots and lots of cats.

"Did you spend much time there?" Gabe asked, and the question brought a hot sting to her eyes.

"My dad died when I was eight." After all this time, the words, the memory, still stung. "He was a family doctor and a child had been sick." Monique Hebert. She'd been six, her fever a hundred and four. Now she was twenty-eight, had four kids of her own. "He'd stayed with her at the clinic until her fever had broken." Closing her eyes, she saw him as he'd been the last time she'd seen him alive, when he'd given her a hug and a kiss, apologized for having to cancel their fishing trip, but promising they would go the next day. "He fell asleep on the way home," she whispered. "Wrapped his car around a tree." And the pain of it, even now, after all this time, made her hands curl more tightly around the wood of the rail.

"I'm sorry," Gabe said, and the edge to his voice said that he really was. Because he knew, too. He knew what it was like to be a child and lose a father.

"We'd moved in with his mother after that." And her own mother had started to drink. Not a lot, just enough to take the edge off, she'd said. "My brother—" Took over. As handyman for their widowed grandmother, support system for their lost mother, surrogate father to a heartbroken little girl.

He'd been ten years old.

"Your brother?" Gabe's voice was oddly quiet. "I didn't realize you had one." Just as she'd not realized he had a sister—because both had been lost to them: one through tragedy, the other through malfeasance.

"He'd tried to make everything okay," she said, seeing Jimmy as he'd been—tall and lanky, with a smile that could melt your heart, but with dark, old-soul eyes that could just as easily break it. "He...grew up too fast."

"I'd say you both did."

"We had to." The way Gabe had had to. "He'd tried to pretend it was okay, that he hadn't wanted to play baseball or go to parties, that going to college hadn't mattered." He'd almost thrown his future away. "But before his senior year—" She laughed softly. "Actually, I don't know what happened. My grandmother took him somewhere one afternoon, and when they'd come back, something had changed. *He* had changed. The next day he'd signed up for the baseball team."

And for a few tenuous months, she'd had her brother back. He'd continued to do too much for all of them, but he'd followed his own dream, as well. He'd pitched the state championship game and run track; he'd dated; he'd kept his grades high. Then he'd gone to New Orleans—

"Evie?"

Her heart kicked hard. Not because Gabe stepped closer, but because of the nickname, the one Jimmy had coined when she'd been just a little girl, without a care in the world other than where her new kitten was, but already convinced beyond reason that her brother hung the moon.

"What happened?" Gabe's voice, so low and gentle and…concerned, made her throat tighten. "What happened to your brother?"

He knew. Without her saying even one word, he knew something had gone wrong. And she hated it, damn it. She hated that this man could read her so easily, read her so well, when he himself was a master of the bluff. Every time she thought she had a handle on him, he went and did something to muddy everything. Like kiss her as if he somehow *needed* to.

Blocking the memory, she lifted her face to the drizzle and welcomed the sting. "I always loved storms," she said. "I'd sit on the front porch with my mom and grandmother and watch them roll in, watch the sky darken and feel the wind pick up." See all the cats scramble under the wood-framed house. "It never occurred to me that anything bad could happen."

That realization had come later.

Gabe came up beside her and propped a hip against the old rail. "You're not going to tell me, are you?"

She knew better than to look at him when everything inside of her felt so raw and exposed. But she turned, anyway, and found him watching her not through the calculating eyes of an attorney on the hunt, but the too-dark eyes of a man on the outside looking in.

"No," she whispered, wrapping her arms around her body.

He should have gotten the hint. But Gabriel Fontenot never did anything she wanted him to do. Instead, he eased the damp strands of hair from her face.

"It's getting colder," he said, but rather than letting his fingers linger against her cheek, he pulled his hand back. "You should come back inside."

What she should do is leave. Gabe could wait for Jack on his own. His friend could give him a ride back to New Orleans. But she stepped toward the glow spilling through the door from inside.

For Jimmy, she told herself as she walked into the main room. For the truth, she amended as Gabe draped an old quilt around her shoulders. She would stay to make sure Jack saw everything, every letter and poem, every picture.

With twilight spilling around them, she let Gabe lead her to the cozy cream-colored sofa with its pattern of peach and buttery yellow hydrangeas—she'd come too far to push him away now, she told herself. She would stay, and she would watch and she would make sure *she* saw everything.

Even what she didn't want to.

Dusk deepened into night. The rain had stopped, leaving only the steady wind to rattle the cabin. And, for the second time in forty-eight hours, Gabe watched her sleep.

She lay curled on the sofa, the soft pink quilt covering most of her body. More of her hair spilled against her cheeks. Her breathing was deep, rhythmic.

She'd fought it. Unlike the night after the warehouse, when she'd dropped off despite his presence in her apartment, this time she'd tried not to fall asleep. She hadn't wanted to let her guard down. But he'd seen the fatigue in her eyes and had settled down in a recliner with the Cameron Monroe book and pretended to read.

Ten minutes later she'd been out.

He wanted to be glad. He should have been glad. With her asleep, there could be no more revelations, no more recollections of a childhood broken by tragedy, of a love of thunderstorms or a brother she'd lost. No more long confused looks.

No more careless, reckless kisses.

But, damn him, he still wanted to touch. It would be so damn easy, too. All he had to do was cross the braided rug and go down on his knees and slide his finger along the line of her jaw…to the smear of green and purple that punched through him like a fist to the gut, visible now after the concealer she'd applied that morning had worn off.

Instead, he kept vigil by the window, where he would see the headlights of Jack's cruiser cut through the night.

But around him, there was only gray. In the sharp, tailored suits Evangeline wore to the courthouse, with her hair swinging in a smooth curtain and her makeup perfect, she looked like a woman who needed nothing or no one. But here, now, dressed like Lilah, with her eyes closed and her lashes sweeping against her cheeks, she looked soft—and oddly lost.

He'd thought that before, in the beginning when he'd found her talking in hushed tones into her cell phone.

She'd turned abruptly, startled, and he would have sworn he saw fear glowing in her eyes. The urge to protect had rocked him.

But then, after he'd discovered her role in the D.A.'s sting, he'd realized he must have walked up on her talking about her strategy or her progress. That's why she'd looked so uncomfortable.

Since then, he'd barely seen her at all. And on those few occasions when he had, all he'd seen was the lies and the deception, the severe suits and lying smile, dark brown eyes that could con as easily as they could seduce.

Until now. Now he saw what he'd not allowed himself to see before, what he still didn't want to see. Watching her sleeping on the sofa, he saw the woman he'd once thought her to be: softer than she wanted most people to realize, warm and courageous, dedicated to truth but with a core of vulnerability she went to great lengths to conceal.

Just like Camille.

Frowning, he looked away from her to the window, but found her there, too, her reflection glowing against the darkness. His sister was out there, too. He knew that, believed it in his heart. He would know if something bad had happened to her. Even when a body had been found in the Everglades matching her description, even as he and Jack had sat silently on the plane racing east, he'd known the blond woman who'd been raped and strangled was not his sister.

She was still out there. Still alone? he wondered. Or had she found someone to trust? Would she have disclosed her secrets, her losses? Did she have someone to gather her close as he'd done so many times—as Evangeline's brother would have done for her, in those dark days following her father's death—to hold her and promise everything would be okay?

He'd lost his sister. Evangeline had lost her brother. They'd both lost fathers….

He brought his hands to his temples and rubbed, but the dull throb didn't lesson. It was past ten. He'd talked to Jack forty-five minutes before. The fire was out, but his grandmother was shaken. Gabe had advised him to stay with her, get her settled. The cottage could wait.

He stood that way, staring into the darkness for an inhumanly long time. Then he went to the kitchen and got a glass of water, pulled the pain pill he'd taken from Evangeline from his pocket. Just this one, he told himself. To dull the edge. He hadn't taken anything prescription in weeks—

He popped it and chugged the water, put the glass into the sink. But he did not return to the main room, to Evangeline. He knew better than to set himself up for a fall. Instead, he went to the bedroom and reread every letter, looking for something they'd missed before. It was close to thirty minutes later before he brought the prom picture with him to the old recliner and flipped it over in his hands.

I'll love you forever.

The words should have brought back the sting of Val's deception. He'd been on the verge of marrying her. But she was gone now, dead, and sweet twisted mercy, when he thought of her, when he tried to remember the life they'd shared or the future she'd claimed to want, it wasn't anger or grief that he felt, but disgust.

Not at her, but himself.

For a man who prided himself on being master of the

bluff, it stung to realize how thoroughly she, in turn, had bluffed him.

He flipped the picture back over and looked at Darci. Someone had bluffed her, too. Someone had played her, plied her with empty words, then discarded her when she no longer fit their purposes,

And he'd bet his life it wasn't the acne-prone boy in the tacky white tuxedo.

Gabe wasn't sure how much time passed, or when his eyes grew heavy. The pain pill, he realized, fighting it, but everything faded and in the darkness of his mind he found her there; Evangeline, dressed in white and easing in and out of the shadows, her hand held out to him….

He came awake hard, jerking up and straining against the shadows. The heat and the smell hit him simultaneously. Coughing, he squinted and bolted to his feet, spun. The kitchen stood empty. The front of the cabin was untouched. But the bedroom door was closed—and he'd left it open.

And from beneath it, leaked whitish gray smoke.

Adrenaline kicked. He ran for the door and put his hand to it, found it hot to the touch. "Sweet Christ," he said as something crashed from within and the first flames licked through the rafters.

"Gabe?" Evangeline rasped, coughing, and he twisted, lunged for the sofa. "Wh-what's happening?"

He reached for her, pulled her into his arms even as he ran. "Fire." At the front door he grabbed the knob and twisted, but nothing happened. Swearing softly, he jerked again; this time harder. But the door wouldn't budge.

"G-Gabe—" she coughed "—c-can't…breathe."

He spun, saw that flames had replaced the smoke

snaking from beneath the bedroom door. There were two windows in the front room. He ran to one of them and flipped the lock.

It didn't budge.

"Gabe!" Evangeline shouted, fisting her hands in his shirt.

He turned just as one of the rafters smashed onto the sofa.

"Son of a bitch!" He ran to the other window and shifted her in his arms, released the lock and jerked.

It didn't move.

"Hang on!" he called over the roar of the fire. They were not going to die in here. She was not going to die. He was not going to let her.

Even if someone wanted them to.

"Stay here," he said, easing her from his arms and positioning her away from the window, away from the glass he was about to send shattering. He reared back, but before he could smash his foot through the window, Evangeline grabbed his arm and pulled him back.

"No!" she rasped, tugging at him even as her hands slid against his damp shirt. "The chairs!"

Smoke filled the room, but squinting against the sting, he twisted and saw what she saw: the old wooden chairs at the small table. Lifting an arm to shield his face, he ran for the chair and grabbed it, snagging an old blanket from the floor near the sofa on the way back to the window.

"Cover up!" he instructed, tossing it toward her. The second the window broke, air would rush in. And the fire would feed.

In seconds the cabin would be engulfed.

"No!" Evangeline barreled into him, slamming her

body against his even as he swung. She yanked the blanket over them both as glass shattered.

The cool air hit with stunning force. Gabe scooped up Evangeline and vaulted through the window, felt the fire lash at his legs. He hit the porch hard and ran, legging it out and leaping to the ground, not stopping until he reached the safety of the trees.

At an old oak he stopped and braced a hand against the trunk, sucked in hard gulps of oxygen. The air was clearer out here, cooler, but each breath seared his lungs. Rasping, he twisted toward the house, saw the flames taunting from the roof and the windows. "Sweet God…"

"Your arms," Evangeline breathed, but before she could touch him, before she could see, he had her on her feet and his hands along her body.

"Tell me where it hurts—"

"No…" The flood of horror was immediate, dark and greedy and drowning out everything else in her eyes, the terror and the pain. The relief. And then she shouted, "No!"

Before he realized her intent, she was pulling away and running back to the house.

"No!" He took off after her, ignoring the dull throb when his foot came down on a cypress knee. "You can't!" At the steps he caught up with her, snagged her by the wrist and pulled her back. "It's too late!"

She twisted against him and pushed. "The evidence! We have to—"

"It's gone." The words, the truth, tore out of him. He kept his hands on her and tried to calm her, didn't want to use force. But their bodies were hot and slick and it was impossible to hold on. "There's nothing left—"

"But how do you know? There could be something—"

"There's not! The fire started there!" In the bedroom. Behind a door he'd left open, but had been closed.

"We have to try!" And she broke from him again, because he'd not held on tightly enough.

This time she ran around the burning house, toward the back. And again he caught her, again dragging her against his body. "Let it go!" He coughed against the smoke searing his throat and his lungs. "There's nothing we can do. It's gone!"

She twisted hard and pivoted to look up at him, to stare up at him with hair falling into her face and soot staining her face, but this time it wasn't fear or alarm that the light of the fire illuminated in her eyes. But shock—and suspicion.

What's in this house could sink the case against Lambert, but you...didn't pretend you hadn't seen anything...

"Evie." Her name scraped on the way out. "No—"

She shoved against him and backed away, never taking her eyes from his. "Those letters—" she coughed "—they could have exonerated Lambert."

They could have. But now they were gone. Destroyed. By a fire set while the lead prosecutor had slept. It would be her word against his. "Don't fall for it," he said, and hated the way his voice went hoarse on the words. "Don't you see?" Because, damn it, he did, and it was more punishingly clear by the second. "This is what they want—just like the night in the warehouse—to pit us against each other."

But she continued to shake her head. "This has nothing to do with the night in the warehouse."

The flames licked higher against the night sky, even

as the rear of the house started to fall in on itself. "Get back!" he warned, but before he could touch her, before he could reach her, she jerked away—and ran.

Chapter 8

Evangeline wasn't a woman to run. Not when her father died. Not when her mother started to drink. Not when Jimmy's employer was found naked and murdered; her brother arrested. Convicted.

By Gabe.

She hadn't run then; she'd stood her ground and fought, done what had to be done, gone to school and learned, prepared, walked into a world that disgusted her, offered a smile to the man who'd put ambition above justice. She'd given him the Trojan Horse of her friendship, then God, somehow she'd given him more, wanted more. Taken more. She'd wanted to reach for him when he hurt, to hold him while he bled.

Even after she'd driven that first knife into his back, she'd sometimes awakened at night with her chest aching, wanting nothing more than to go to Gabe, to put her arms around him and tell him she was sorry. Promise him everything would be okay.

But she had not run, had not let all those nasty, swirling shades of gray sway her from the course she'd charted. She'd pressed on, and she'd found her way back into Gabe's life.

Now she welcomed the slap of the cool night air as she ripped at the tangled vines of Spanish moss. She tried to breathe, to think. She knew that Gabe followed. She could hear him, feel him.

Because of the fire, she told herself. That's why she ran. Because the house had started to collapse, sending smoldering debris against the night sky. It had nothing to do with Gabe. Or the truth. The lie.

She'd slept. She hadn't just lowered her guard, she'd let it crumble around her and, for the second time in two days, she'd closed her eyes to Gabriel Fontenot. The first time he'd tossed her apartment. This time, he'd destroyed crucial evidence.

It had to have been him. Nothing else made sense. She'd marveled at the way Gabe had taken the poems and letters in stride, even as their mere existence dealt a significant blow to his dream of bringing down Marcel Lambert.

But now they were gone, every tender word, every promise and vow, every snapshot of a relationship that had been painted as sordid and abusive.

Because of a fire set while she slept.

That's why she had to stop. Because when she'd backed away from Gabe and felt the suspicion leak through every cell of her body, when she'd lifted her eyes to his, the horrified glitter she'd seen staring back at her, the raw, boiling hurt, had stripped her to the bone.

And against every scrap of logic and reason, in violation of everything she knew about right and wrong and survival, she'd wanted to believe him. That he hadn't set the fire, hadn't destroyed the evidence. Hadn't tampered with the jury that stole her brother's future, hadn't made sure juror number three never had the chance to disclose what she knew.

That he wasn't the man she'd always believed him to be—but the man she wanted him to be.

That's why she threw on the brakes as the first sirens sounded. That's why she stopped, would not let herself run anymore. Not from this man, or the dangerous truth he represented.

"Evie—" his voice was low and hoarse and…urgent, and it slipped through her with visceral force "—don't do this."

This is what they want, he'd reasoned before. *Just like the night in the warehouse…to pit us against each other.*

But there *was* no one from the night at the warehouse. She was the one who'd staged that meet to gain entrance back into his life. But if she was the one who'd staged that night…

What kind of man do you think I am? he'd asked earlier. And with the fire spitting against the night sky and the red lights flashing closer, the truth sliced deeper than the guilt.

He was a man who would do anything to get what he wanted.

"Please," he said now, and with the word he touched her arm but did not tighten his fingers, did not try to make her turn.

She did that on her own. "Don't," she whispered. Touch her. Not with his hands or his voice, his words.

He winced, as if she'd taken a knife to his gut. "I know you're scared," he said. And, God help her, it hurt to hear his voice, so rough from the smoke and the fire. "But you need to trust me."

Need. To trust. Him.

"I fell asleep." He gritted out the words as headlights cut through the clearing, followed by a fire engine. "The smoke woke me."

It was hard, but she resisted the urge to step closer and lift a hand to his face, wipe the smear of blood from his cheek.

"I want Marcel Lambert," he added, "but not like this."

Her heart kicked hard. She stood there staring up at him, at the shirt that was now filthy and torn and hanging open, the sleeves rolled up, revealing the dried blood against his forearms.

"I would never risk your life!" he said, and the words sounded torn from somewhere inside of him.

But she did not let herself sway, just lifted her chin as she did in the courtroom when a witness offered a pile of lies.

Behind them a squad car screeched into the clearing and the door swung open, a man shot out. "Gabriel!"

He stiffened but did not turn, just looked at her through the most scorched-earth eyes she'd ever seen.

"Jesus, Gabriel!" the tall man shouted from behind them, and against the glow of the fire she could see him sprinting toward what remained of the house.

"My God…he thinks we're in—"

But Gabe was already running back. "*Jacques,* no!" he shouted as the other man vanished from sight.

Within seconds, Gabe, too, was gone.

Horrified, Evangeline started after them, trying not

to trip on the maze of roots. But the second she rounded the house, she stopped. Because she saw them, Gabe and the other man, staggering from the smoke-filled front door. Two firefighters rushed toward them, as two more dragged a hose toward the front porch.

Then everything slowed. She watched, couldn't make herself move, not when cool, calm, always in control Gabriel Fontenot pulled the man he'd called Jacques into his arms. Not briefly, like men tended to do, but hard and full. Like brothers.

They pulled back abruptly and squared off…again like brothers. *"Merde, frère,"* Jack muttered, "you damn near got me killed."

"Sorry about that," Gabe said, and then the strangest thing happened. They laughed. And thumped each other on the back.

The fascination came on a near-violent whisper. Evangeline stood in silent witness and watched, felt her heart break all over again. Jimmy had had a best friend. Seth. They'd been like brothers.

But Seth was gone now, killed in a freak motorcycle accident. And she'd had to tell Jimmy. She'd had to sit in that brightly lit little room at Angola and tell her brother that his best friend had died. Alone. She'd had to sit there and watch him cry, unable to do anything— except this.

From the recently arrived cars two men strode toward Gabe and Jack, while a woman in a ponytail ran. She got there first, launching herself into Gabe's arms and hugging him hard. Then the men joined them, both tall and with the kind of commanding presence that made Evangeline's breath catch, even from a distance, followed by a second woman she'd not noticed initially.

Gabe stood with his back to her, his arm around the woman in the ponytail, encircled by the rest of the group. He never turned back, not even a glance. But the women did, first the tall blonde, then the one with the ponytail. And the accusation in her eyes sliced through Evangeline even from twenty feet away.

The jagged realization of how hideously her plan had backfired stunned her. Gabriel Fontenot was not her friend. She was not part of his inner circle, not his confidante. She'd come into his life with one purpose and one purpose only: to bring him down.

But she'd never counted on his smile. Or his touch, the way everything inside her warmed and wanted. She'd been wrong to think she could pose as his friend and keep herself apart from him. Wrong to think there would be no gray.

Now she knew, and as she watched the woman in the ponytail wipe the soot from Gabe's face, she ignored the way her own throat went tight.

She wasn't sure how long she watched before the blonde broke from the group and strode toward her. She was a striking woman, Evangeline noted as she neared. Even without a shred of makeup. Her hair was long and loose around her face, her gait confident but comfortable.

"I'm Savannah," she said as she approached, and the name clicked. *Savannah.* Fiancée to Gabe's cousin, Cain, a woman thought dead for almost two years. Were it not for Gabe, Cain surely would have gone to prison for a murder he not only hadn't committed, but a murder that hadn't *happened.* "I'll be taking you back to New Orleans."

The measured words sliced through Evangeline. She told herself not to react, not to hurt. She was the one who'd pushed Gabe away. She was the one who'd accused him of starting the fire, destroying the evidence. Because that's what the man she'd always believed him to be would do.

But in accusing him of destroying evidence, she, in turn, had destroyed the fragile bonds she'd been working hard to restore. "Thank you," she said, forcing a smile.

But Savannah frowned. "Are you cold?" she asked, starting to shrug out of her jacket. "You can—"

"I'm fine."

And with that Evangeline let Savannah lead her to a sleek little black Mercedes convertible. She knew better than to look back, knew what she would see: the firefighters working against the collapsing house and Gabe circled by his friends.

But she looked anyway.

And saw Gabe. Standing with his feet shoulder width apart, tall and untouchable against the fading flames, his shirt torn, his jeans covered by soot. But somehow he still looked like the man she'd seen dominate countless courtrooms.

Even with his back to her.

"Gabriel…hold still."

The command in his cousin's voice stopped him. She may have been the only female present and smaller by many inches and pounds, but he'd learned long ago not to cross Saura Robichaud. She possessed the same stubborn streak as her male cousins, just with a whole lot prettier packaging. Which gave her a whole lot more power.

If he snatched his arm from her, she'd simply track him across the room.

So, instead, Gabe forced himself to keep straddling

one of the chairs at Jack's dining-room table. Jaw clenched, he glared at the alcohol-drenched cotton balls Saura used to clean the dried blood against the series of scrapes and scratches along his forearm. "Ow!" he forced himself to growl, because *ow* was absolutely not what he *wanted* to say. White flashes streaked across his vision. "That stings."

Almost blithely, Saura went for a deep cut against his wrist and squeezed the cotton, letting the alcohol drip. "Healing usually does." Her voice danced somewhere between maternal and demonic. If he didn't know better, he would have sworn she was enjoying this a little too much.

Then again, he wasn't sure he knew better.

"Maybe you'll think twice before smashing out windows with your bare arms again," she added, going for another scrape.

"I'll make note of that for the next time someone tries to kill me," he said drily.

This time she stopped. And this time she looked up at him. With a single long braid draped over her shoulder, she looked deceptively harmless. From the dark glow in her Robichaud eyes, he knew she was anything but.

"Well, well," she drawled. "Look who's back, sugary insolence and all." Then she smiled and bent toward him, kissed him on the cheek. "If I'd known all it was going to take was a little fire—"

"I'll just bet you would have," he said drily.

"Careful," her fiancé called, emerging from Jack's kitchen, and though D'Ambrosia's tone held warning, his eyes gleamed. "She doesn't need any encouragement."

"She has an evil streak, that one," Cain agreed, join-

ing them with a large storage crate in his arms. He set
it on the table just as Jack emerged from the back room
with a smaller box. "But then," Cain added, "you already know that."

He did. And for a disjointed moment twenty years
fell away and they were kids again, Cain and Jack and
Saura, himself, gathered around a kitchen table and
studying his father's notes.

And Camille. She'd been there then.

"At least, I thought you were back," Saura said, and
with another drizzle of alcohol, time surged forward and
Gabe jerked, snatching his arm away.

But Saura had already seen, and she already knew.
"I know," she whispered. "She should be here."

And then he couldn't sit any longer, couldn't just
wait at the kitchen table while Saura tended to his
arm, not when Marcel Lambert was once again playing
puppet-master to their lives. The bastard had already
taken too much.

"It's all a game to him," he said, shoving back from
the chair and standing, pivoting toward the antique buffet
on the other side of the room. Through the mirror he saw
them all watching him—Saura with concern and Cain
with the same contempt that coursed through Gabe; Jack,
a dark combination of regret and anticipation. Gabe's
family wasn't the only family that had been destroyed that
night.

"Everything," he said. The missing files from his courthouse office and the chance meeting with Evangeline
at the warehouse, the waitress who'd never shown. She
was probably enjoying a vacation in the Bahamas somewhere, courtesy of her boss, Marcel Lambert. "He knew
I was coming to Wild Berry." Just as the bastard seemed

to know everything else. "He wanted me to find the house," he added, as he'd speculated earlier with Evie.

Evie.

Christ, he could still see her as she'd turned to face him, the way she'd backed away as if she were afraid—*a-freaking-fraid*—of him touching her. She'd stood with her hair in her face, trying to catch her breath, staring at him with eyes far, far too dark and skin far too pale. Any trace of the woman from earlier in the evening, the woman who'd pushed up on her toes and met his mouth with her own…gone.

"The fire," he said, spinning toward Jack, standing with an old journal in his hand, "in your grandmother's neighborhood. That was no accident." It was a diversion. "He knew I'd stay at the house, knew if enough time went by we'd fall asleep waiting—"

Jack put down the old notebook, one that had once belonged to *his* father. "If it was anyone else, I'd say no freaking way."

Saura let the bloodied cotton ball fall from her fingers. "But it's not anyone else."

Cain retrieved an old sketch from the storage box he'd carried down from the attic. Even from several feet away, Gabe could see the image that had captivated them as children. "*Mais,* he has made one very big mistake."

There were those who would have said it was an inopportune time to smile—Marcel Lambert had either just tried to kill him, or set him up—but Gabe met Cain's gaze and felt the slow, deliberate curve of his mouth originate from somewhere deep and dark. Despite the passing of almost a quarter of a century, Lambert was the same cunning bastard he'd always been. A man who'd used his wealth and celebrity status to skate outside the law.

But Gabe was different. Cain and Saura were different. Jack was different. Camille...

They weren't kids anymore.

And they weren't going to let the son of a bitch win.

Gabe returned to the table and looked at the drawing Cain had set down. Jack and Saura closed in with him, the way they'd done as kids. The overhead light, illuminated the detailed drawing of his father's passion: a fabled piece of stained glass smuggled out of France by two children during the French Revolution.

The children had been Robichauds—the stained glass from their family chapel in Brittany.

As a child, the stories had fascinated: a region of France renowned for healing, sacred waters, holy wells, fields of standing stones and a stained-glass window shrouded in mystery.

Now a man, Gabe saw the legends for what they were: a dangerous obsession and a tailor-made bluff. A few well-placed whispers, a rumor here, an allegation there and Marcel Lambert would come looking—as he had the night Camille had seen her father gunned down.

"Gabe—" Saura said, and in her eyes he saw a worry that touched him in ways very few people could.

"I know." Stirring up a hornets' nest was dangerous. He knew that. His plan could backfire, blow up in his face—or fall flat.

But he was done being played. The images flashed hard, not just of Marcel Lambert and the brother who'd set his sights on Saura several weeks before, but of Val who'd claimed to love him, but had only been using him. *Of Evangeline.*

Black-and-white, she'd said that night at the warehouse. *That's all you see, isn't it?*

He still wasn't sure how she'd made his mantra sound like a crime. There was no such thing as a little bit guilty—either someone was, or wasn't. Shades of gray were nothing more than flimsy shadows thrown up to distort reality.

What do you want from me? she'd asked, and, damn it, he would have sworn her voice had broken. *For me to tell you I'm sorry? I've—* Her eyes had darkened, and, like a fool, he'd had the dangerous urge to reach for her. *I've already done that.* More than once. *It didn't do much good.*

He had touched her then, lifted his hand to her face and skimmed his thumb along her cheekbone. *You sure you want to know what I want?*

He crushed the memory and focused on the drawing, on now and Lambert. He had a big charity event in less than twenty-four hours. He would be strutting through the aquarium like a genteel, innocent son of the South. His tuxedo would be ivory, Gabe knew. It always was.

"By this time tomorrow night," he said, looking first at Saura, then D'Ambrosia and Cain, lingering on Jack. "Lambert will be on his way down."

A dark light glittered in Jack's eyes, but he said nothing. None of them did. They all knew what needed to be done—and what hung in the balance.

But then Cain's cell phone rang and he reached for it and turned away, talking quietly before handing it to Gabe. "It's Vannah," he mouthed.

"You on your way back?" he asked when he brought the phone to his ear.

"Yes," she said. "I've just left Evangeline's."

"Good." That was all he let himself say.

"I took her by Dr. Collette's, like you asked," Savannah said, answering a question he hadn't asked. "Physically she's fine, might have a sore throat for a few days from smoke inhalation—"

He glanced at his watch, saw the hour nearing 4:00 a.m. "What time do you think you'll be back here?"

"Gabe."

Because the censure in her voice stung, he ignored it. "We're going over details—"

"She asked about you."

Four little words. That was all. But they went through him like a shot of cheap whiskey. He stiffened, felt his jaw go tight—felt four pairs of eyes watching him. Swearing, he turned and walked into Jack's oddly out-of-place gourmet kitchen, tried not to gag on the scent of dark-roast coffee.

"Gabe?" Savannah asked over the static. "You there?"

He brought his fingers to his temple. The pounding of earlier in the evening had faded, leaving a dull ache. If he hadn't taken that pain pill— "I'm here." But he didn't let himself ask—didn't want to know. "Thanks for taking her back. Cain will fill you in—"

"My God, Gabriel, aren't you even going to ask?"

"There's nothing to ask."

"What about 'What did she ask?'" Savannah shot back. "'Is she scared?' or 'Is she okay?'"

"You already told me she's okay."

"I said she checked out fine with Collette," Savannah corrected. "Physically. But I never said she's okay."

The quick brutal slice caught him by surprise.

"Because she's not okay," Savannah went on, before he could ask—or tell—her to stop. "She did a great job of hiding it, but she's scared, Gabe. She's worried about you. Worried about your arm and your headache and what you're going to do next—"

"Savannah, stop." He didn't want to hear it, didn't want to imagine. "I don't need you to—"

"When you asked me to drive her back to New Orleans," Savannah rolled right on, "I knew who she was and what she'd done to you, and I didn't understand how you'd let yourself end up in the middle of nowhere with *her,* of all people. For all I knew *she* torched the evidence just to finish what she started last fall."

Savannah's insinuation slammed into him. He stood there as a flash flood of nasty pieces swirled around him, falling into a disgustingly tidy picture. Gabe had no doubt Lambert was stringing him along, setting him up, planning to take Gabe out before he could take Lambert out.

Recruiting Evangeline would be a stroke of genius.

Chapter 9

"No." The word ground through Gabe. He'd seen the look in Evangeline's eyes when he'd talked of Camille and his father, of loss—when she'd talked of her brother and her father and loss. He'd kissed her and tasted the same yearning that had been there all those months before. But also something new and different, a fear and uncertainty, a tentativeness that had almost sent him to his knees. And then later, after the fire, when she'd turned to him and looked up at him, he'd seen horror in her eyes—

"No," he said again, this time softer, and then he realized that Savannah was talking, had been all along.

"...spooked, Gabe, but not because she's working for someone else. I saw something in her eyes that I used to see every morning in the mirror, a struggle between caution and longing. You have no idea what that's like, Gabe, to stare at a mountain of evidence that tells you to stay away from someone, but to want them anyway…."

He closed his eyes. Hard. Because he did know, damn it. He knew too damn well.

"Gabe…" Savannah said, and he wasn't sure whether it was disappointment or admonishment in her voice, but slowly he opened his eyes and stared out at the shadows beyond the window, seeing another window…back in New Orleans, in which a set of floral wind chimes hung.

"Drive safe," he said, then disconnected the call.

She barely slept. After crawling into bed shortly before four, Evangeline was out by six and in the shower for the second time. But no matter how much warm water rained down on her, the acrid residue of smoke wouldn't fade.

She tried to review her notes about the Lambert case, but her mind wouldn't stay in one place.

She fed Simon then called juror number eight to see if he could meet earlier, but reached only his voice mail.

By 9:00 a.m. she was on her way to Angola, only to be told upon arrival that Jimmy had declined her visit.

Early afternoon found her back in New Orleans, checking her voice messages as she drove Uptown— and listening to the district attorney rant. "I don't know where you are, Angie, but I need you to call me. The press is crawling all over me," Vince Arceneaux said. "They want to know about the fire."

She eased off the gas and turned down the quiet tree-lined street.

"Of course, to tell them about the fire, I would actually need to know something," Vince rolled on. "Like if you were really there and what in holy kingdom you were doing."

Evangeline bit down on her lip, knew she couldn't avoid her boss forever. Or the truth.

"Because I damn well know you're going to tell me Gabe was not there with you. That he did not get his hands on critical evidence—and that you absolutely did not leave him alone with it."

Her throat tightened as she saw the house, a reno-vated Victorian with a small screened porch. Two cars sat parked in the street beneath the canopy of an old oak. The sexy little convertible she recognized; the sleek BMW she did not.

"We'll talk tonight," Vince promised. "At the Aquar-ium." That was where the fund-raiser was being held, the renowned tourist attraction that had survived Katrina with little physical damage, but had lost a significant portion of its aquatic life when a backup generator had failed.

Now again functional, the aquarium had yet to return to its former splendor, but the city was working on it. A portion of the proceeds raised through Marcel's gala would go to acquiring more species, as well as efforts to attract dislocated citizens back to the city.

Marcel's philanthropy, it appeared, did not discrimi-nate. He clearly wanted his well-manicured hand in every effort that could provide glory—and good press.

"Don't be late," Vince said in that smoothed, cultured voice of his. "And, Angie? I trust you won't say a word to the press until you talk to me."

She eased Jimmy's prized '67 Mustang to a stop on the opposite side of the street. Even if Gabe saw, he would not know it was her behind the darkly tinted win-

dows. She'd made sure of that. She'd kept the car in a
garage, only let Gabe see the sports coupe she'd purchased when she moved to New Orleans.

For ten years every step she'd taken, *every breath,*
had been with only one goal in mind: to prove Gabriel
Fontenot had used his family's wealth to make sure he
won his first case as an assistant district attorney. She'd
promised Jimmy and her mother that one day this whole
nightmare would be over.

And now, at last, she had the means to levy a severe
blow against Gabriel Fontenot. A few words to the
D.A. and Gabe would be the one facing a criminal
investigation—

Gabe, who'd lost his father and his sister, who'd
grown from boy to man amidst the devastation of one
single bullet. Who'd never given up looking for Camille,
never stopped believing…

Gabe, who'd chased her through the shadows of the
old warehouse and tackled her, but who'd scooped her
into his arms and run for help the second he'd realized
he'd hurt her.

Gabe, whom she'd betrayed, but who'd taken her
face into his hands, anyway, and kissed her with a need
that stunned.

Gabe, who'd lunged for her through the smoke-
infested darkness of Marcel's cabin, who'd shielded
her as he'd smashed out the window, then'd picked her
up and run to safety.

Gabe, who'd stood against the fire ravaging the little house, his face covered in soot and his arms covered in scratches, staring down at her through those
dark, wounded eyes as if she'd accused him of some
heinous crime.

Gabe, who'd turned from her, walked from her, hadn't looked back.

Reality cut hard and deep, and with a determination that oozed like poison, she swallowed against the emotion and eased down on the gas pedal.

Gabe, who would hate her the second he realized who she really was and what she'd wanted all along.

She had to quit doing this to herself. Stop seeing Gabe as a series of disjointed snapshots. She had to focus on the black-and-white, rather than the gray she'd exploited for as long as she could remember. The end justified the means, she'd told herself. A few lies, a smile when she felt like crying, a hand offered in friendship when in reality she'd wanted to slap... As long as she was helping Jimmy, the steps along the way didn't matter.

Until her attempts to fake a friendship with Gabe turned into something dangerously real.

And now, God help her, her own emotions closed in on her like the suffocating smoke from the night before, bringing with it the sobering realization that for one of the few times in her life, she wanted to be wrong.

It was all so very civilized. Marcel strolled toward Evangeline the second she stepped inside the crowded lobby of the Aquarium of the Americas. The perfect genteel host, he nodded and smiled at the well-dressed guests. The lines of his tanned face were easy, his dark eyes glowing with welcome. His tuxedo was ivory.

Finding a practiced smile, she watched Marcel close the distance between them. His wife walked by his side, her hair perfectly coiffed, her makeup understated, her jewelry elegant and tasteful. Her smile glued in place.

She had her hand tucked inside her husband's arm, as if she wasn't about to let him go.

The irony streamed through Evangeline on so many levels.

"Evangeline," Marcel greeted in a smooth, polished voice, with just a hint of Cajun. When he appeared on daytime talk shows to share recipes and promote the city, the accent had a mysterious way of deepening. "So nice of you to join us."

She lifted her hand as he reached for it. "I wouldn't miss it for the world."

"You look lovely," Caroline added, sweeping her gaze along Evangeline's simple black dress and estate-sale jewelry, the stilettos she'd picked up on clearance last fall.

"Thank you." From simple appearances, it would be impossible to know Marcel Lambert faced murder charges—and that the only reason he walked free was because the judge had granted bail against her vehement protests. Their choreography was that flawless.

"You do, as well," she said, cringing as a photographer materialized.

"Smile," Marcel said, and before she could even move, he slipped an arm around her waist and the camera flashed—and the image was captured, that of the murder suspect and the prosecuting attorney, together. Smiling.

And, without doubt, she knew Lambert had achieved his goal in sashaying over to her.

"You absolutely must try Marci's shrimp remoulade," Caroline was saying. "And his crabmeat cheesecake." Her smile turned dreamy. "With pecan crust."

"Sounds fabulous," Evangeline said, as if there

wasn't even the remotest chance this man had come within minutes of having her killed the night before.

"Angie." The urbane voice came from behind her. She turned, found Vince closing in fast. Reaching her, he put a hand to the small of her back and exchanged pleasantries with the Lamberts.

"I'm sure you'll understand if I steal my girl for a few minutes," he concluded, and Evangeline felt herself stiffen. She knew her boss had chosen the words for show, as he did everything. But the good-old-boy posturing made her cringe.

Gabe had never—

"There's something we need to…discuss," Vince said, earning a garbled laugh from Marcel.

"I'll just bet there is." More smiles, more falsities, then he and Caroline swept away. Evangeline watched them pose for another picture, all Southern hospitality and smiles—

And saw him.

He stood toward the back of the room, next to one of the saltwater aquariums. The soft blue lighting used for the wall-sized tank provided an eerie backdrop for the way he stood so tall and unmoving in a tuxedo of all black, his body, his eyes, everything hard and fixed.

On her.

An entire room separated them, waiters scurrying around with trays on their hands, women in black and silver and gold, clusters of men. But all of that faded— the murmur of voices and the soft strains of jazz, the scent of Cajun delicacies and perfume—leaving only Gabe. Standing there, where he so categorically should not be.

At Marcel's fund-raiser.

Watching her.

The way he'd refused to do the night before.

"Angie?" Vince asked, and started to turn toward the back of the room.

She intercepted him before he spied Gabe. "You don't see a waiter, do you? I'd love a glass of chardonnay."

Vince signaled for one of the staff. A young man in a pristine white jacket hurried over, allowing Vince to pluck two stems.

"If I didn't know better," he said after the waiter slipped into the crowd, "I'd think you were avoiding me."

"Nonsense." She smiled up at Vince, knew she couldn't chance a look beyond his shoulder, couldn't risk him following her gaze. But she felt Gabe, anyway. Felt the dull blade of his scrutiny scrape over every inch of her body.

"About this fire," Vince was saying, frowning. "I need to know what happened." He stepped slightly to his left, but it was enough to see the second man. And the third. The fourth.

They were all there—not just Gabe, but Cain and Jack and John D'Ambrosia. All tall and grim-faced, all dressed in black tuxedos. All strategically placed and standing unnaturally still. Watching.

Not her, though. But, Lambert.

Her heart kicked hard and the truth sliced deep. An ambush, she realized. Gabe was not here for her, not here because of her.

He was here for Marcel Lambert.

He didn't want to watch her. He didn't want to look. He was not here for her. But from the second he'd spotted her chatting with Lambert in his goddamn ivory tuxedo, when Lambert had brought her hand to his mouth, the slow boil had taken over.

He watched her now—talking with the district attorney, not a hair out of place, her makeup flawless and her sexy little black dress hugging in all the right places—and forced himself to see the evidence right in front of him.

Someone had set him up. Someone wanted to see him fall for destroying the notes and letters and pictures; to use him to set Lambert free.

And that someone was Lambert himself. That was how a snake operated. That was how he got away with murder.

But his choice of weapons…

Gabe watched the movers and shakers of New Orleans parade around him, watched Lambert laughing with a city councilwoman and a reporter for a news show, then Evangeline with Vince. Talking to him. So cool and calm and collected…as if she hadn't almost been killed the night before.

Everything inside of Gabe tightened at the realization, but he forced himself to hold on to it, forced himself to consider the possibility. The attorney in him knew that Evangeline could be a pawn. Lambert could have recruited her and sent her after him, assigned her to infiltrate his life, just as Val had been assigned to infiltrate his life.

The comparison ground through him. He watched a waiter with a tray of red wine, wanted so damn badly to flag him down. But did not allow himself to move. A drink wouldn't change anything. He knew that, knew he had to force himself to see, no matter how much he hated *what* he saw. He'd fallen for Val's insecurity act, had actually felt responsible for her. When she'd cried, he'd held her. When she'd claimed he was all she had, he'd believed her. And when he'd brought critical information home from the office, she'd taken it, exploited it.

"He sees you," Jack whispered through the earpiece, and Gabe resisted the urge to turn and look, to hold Lambert's gaze and let him know in no uncertain terms that he was on to him.

But that wasn't what tonight was about. Tonight was about letting Lambert feel in control. Tonight was about backing him deeper into a corner he had no idea was coming. "Keep on him," Gabe instructed Jack, then turned and casually made his way toward the back of the aquarium, where an open-air patio overlooked the river. He plucked a stem of champagne on the way, smiling and nodding as if he had every right to be there.

"Stop her."

The emphatically whispered words were not meant for him. But he stopped and turned, anyway, saw her. She remained with the D.A. That had not changed. But she no longer looked untouchable. No longer looked untouched. He saw her mouth work, saw her try to slip away from Arceneaux, but Savannah swooped in with perfect timing and reached for her hands, just as Cain closed in on Vince.

Her eyes hardened with an odd combination of frustration and dread, but Gabe ripped his gaze away and strode from the room that reeked of perfume and cooking oil—and deception.

Working his way through the humid rain-forest exhibit, he followed the path to the decoratively lit patio. Tiki torches swayed in the cool breeze. Strings of chili-pepper party lights illuminated the shrubbery like garish Christmas decorations. He walked amid it all and positioned himself with his back to the door.

The perfect bait, he knew, could not be resisted.

Almost like clockwork, footsteps sounded behind him. A man's, he could tell from the heavy gait. Not a woman's.

Not Evangeline's.

He allowed himself no guilt, not even as his last sight of her flashed through his mind, of her trying to make her way to him, to stop him. Of Savannah stopping her, instead. Of the way Evangeline had looked at him, as if she saw a train wreck coming, but there wasn't a damn thing she could do stop it.

Which there wasn't.

"So glad you could join us tonight, Gabriel."

The deceptively benign words fell around Gabe like a hand of aces. He didn't smile, though, didn't give any indication that Lambert had just swallowed his bait, hook, line and sinker. He didn't even turn. He merely gathered his cards close and stood there, looking out at the river while Marcel's cigarette smoke swirled closer.

The man who'd lived a charmed life while Gabe's father lay interred in darkness came to stand beside him—close without touching—and did as Gabe did, looked out over the river. "I can only imagine how difficult it must be," he commented blandly, "being here among your peers and the press, seeing the way they look at you. Knowing that they know…everything."

Everything. The word dangled in the breeze, carrying with it the whisperings that followed Gabe every-*where:* about Val and his suspension from the D.A.'s office, the handgun found in his house, about his drinking and need for pain pills. And just as when he knew a jury was turning his way, Gabe blanked the slow gleam of satisfaction—for such a smooth operator, Marcel Lambert was ridiculously predictable.

"That why you're out here, Gabriel? You needed to get away from it all…find some fresh air?"

Watching a barge on the river, Gabe brought the

champagne flute to his mouth and sipped. "Is there something you wanted?" he asked. "I've already tried the oysters."

Lambert's laugh was smooth and polished, so pathetically civilized. "Let me call someone to come get you," he offered. "Your mama maybe? I've been meaning to call Ruthanne, tell her how glad I am that dead girl in Florida didn't turn out to be our little Camille."

Gabe refused to allow his jaw to tighten, knew Marcel was simply attacking from another angle. But the nasty jab unlocked the memory, and for a brutal second he saw the sheet-draped body on the table. He and Jack had looked at the sheet a long, long time. The description had matched. The young woman had been blond and pretty, with green eyes and delicate features, freckles. She'd been five foot six, just like Camille. The tattoos on the body had not been there before, but a lot could happen in ten years.

She'd died a hard, violent death.

Gabe would never forget the way his knees had wanted to buckle when the coroner had pulled back the sheet and they'd seen the young woman's face. He'd crossed himself. Jack had just stood there, staring....

"But wait a minute, your mama's out of town, isn't she?" Lambert asked, as if he gave a flat red damn. But then, that was the game he'd been playing with Gabe's family for over twenty years. "Heard she had some trouble."

Gabe put the champagne flute onto the rail, kept his face expressionless. As a young man, when he'd first joined the district attorney's office, he'd let Lambert's thinly veiled taunts get to him.

But he was a man now and he knew how to play the game.

"Did you have a point with all this?" he asked in a tight voice, allowing Lambert to think he had the upper hand.

"Just worried about you, son, that's all. After everything you've been through…"

Again Gabe let Lambert's comment dangle between them, let the silence stir with the breeze rustling the strings of lights. All the while he looked out into the darkness, where a brightly lit paddleboat-turned-floating-casino glided to the dock following one of its requisite cruises.

"She's so quiet," Gabe commented. Still. Like a spider waiting in her web. "The river," he clarified. Seemingly benign, wide and grand and constant, running like an old friend through the city. Through everything. "It would be easy to be deceived, wouldn't it?" he mused. "Easy to forget what she's capable of."

The tip of Lambert's cigarette glowed against the night. "Perhaps." Lowering his arm to the rail, he let his thin cigarette dangle between his fingers. "*Mais,* she has not won yet, has she?" he said with the misplaced arrogance of someone who thought they'd gotten away with murder. *Twice.* "No matter how hard she's tried, no matter how much collateral damage has fallen, I am still here."

Gabe savored the slow, sweet rush of adrenaline. They were so not talking about the river.

"Borrowed time," he muttered. "Isn't that what the government says?" That one day the river and the swamp would reclaim the city that care forgot and she would fade to nothing but memory.

This time Lambert laughed. "Posturing," he boasted. "It'll never happen."

Gabe strummed his fingers along the rail. "My father always said—" he started, but then Jack's voice was there, an urgent whisper through the earpiece: "You're about to have company."

"Your father said what?"

Gabe turned toward Lambert, giving himself a better look at the path leading from the rain-forest exhibit. "*Never* is a dangerous word," he said. "Almost like asking for—" he saw her then, saw her emerge from the heavily foliaged path, practically at a dead run or, at least, as close to a run as her strappy heels and sinful little dress would allow "—trouble."

She stopped. "Gabe—" she mouthed without voice, and, damn it, he didn't understand what he saw in her eyes, the horror and the suspicion, the dread. It was almost as if—

Almost as if she'd been afraid of what she might find.

The urge to go to her ground through him, to pull her behind him and away from Lambert, where the other man couldn't touch her, couldn't so much as see her.

Couldn't use her.

"Well, well," Lambert drawled, because he had turned and he had seen. "This evening just keeps getting more interesting by the second, doesn't it?"

Something dark and punishing drove Gabe. He strode toward Evangeline and reached for her, touched her even though he'd told himself that could never happen again. "You need to go."

She didn't move. "What are you doing?" she whispered fiercely. "Do you have any idea—"

"I have plenty of ideas," he snapped before she could finish. And they all pushed in on him, hard and brutal and jagged. Evangeline and Gabe and Marcel were three players on a stage, each with their own unrehearsed script.

"Gabe—" she started, but he didn't let her finish, not when he had one more card to play. He tugged her toward him and stabbed his hands into her hair, tilting her face toward his.

Then he crushed his mouth to hers and kissed her.

Chapter 10

Everything blurred. Evangeline told herself to pull away, but shock held her immobile. Gabe's hands were on her face, not roughly like the glitter in his eyes had promised, but with a gentleness that ripped through her. Too many nights she'd jerked herself from the shadows of her dreams, unable to forget the way he'd been touching her, the gentleness and the hunger.

He touched her that way now, when he shouldn't be touching her at all. Not after the finality with which he'd walked away the night before, not with Marcel Lambert looking on. She'd braced herself, had been certain he was going to drag her away from his clandestine meeting with Marcel.

Instead, he'd reached for her, and in that one hazy moment, everything Evangeline thought she knew crumbled. Confusion bled and need burned. Denial shattered.

She knew the kiss had nothing to do with dreams or nightmares and everything to do with the scene she'd just walked in on. But there was something in the slant of Gabe's mouth that had not been there before, not in her dreams, not in the stolen moments the night before. Now there was frustration and now there was sorrow. But it wasn't a hard kiss, wasn't unrestrained. There amid the taste of champagne, she found a tenderness and a regret that almost destroyed.

And then she knew, then she realized. As his hands tangled in her hair, it wasn't tenderness that she tasted. It was deliberateness, the cool, cold calculation of a man executing his bluff.

She pushed against him. "Don't—"

But Gabe only smiled. "Why not, *catin?* Isn't that what you've been wanting all along? To lure me in—"

Moments before, everything blurred. Now it stopped. "What are you—"

Gabe didn't let her finish, just turned toward Marcel. "She's all yours," he said, and started to walk away.

The truth cut from all directions, the punishing possibility that Gabe thought she had something going with Lambert. That she worked for him, that she was the one who'd been sent to sabotage the evidence and frame Gabe, to destroy his career and his vendetta. "Gabe—" she said, but the freezing look in his eyes stopped her. Because she knew. She'd walked into this trap. She'd set herself up for this fall. She *had* lied to Gabe. She *had* tried to lure him in. She *had* wanted only to use him.

And now, God, she realized that somewhere along the line she'd made a huge mistake—but she wasn't sure when. When she'd let Gabe touch her and felt the awakening inside, the longing? When she'd found herself walking into her own trap and responding to the man she'd trained herself to hate?

Or further back, in the beginning, when she'd first targeted Gabe, first believed he'd tampered with the jury that had taken Jimmy's future from him?

"You've got this wrong," she said, because it was important to her that he know the truth, that he not believe she'd been part of a seedy alliance with the man who'd killed his father.

But the indifference in Gabe's eyes told her it was too late. The lies were already there. The betrayals and the deception. She was the one who'd been unable to answer one simple question: *What kind of man do you think I am?*

"Do I?" he asked. But before she could answer Saura and John D'Ambrosia strolled in from the rain-forest exhibit. Their fluid body language was that of lovers, but the gleam in their eyes warned there was nothing casual about their appearance.

The silence lasted only a heartbeat. As a horn blew from the barge on the river, Marcel Lambert laughed. "Ah," he said. "The rescue party. How quaint."

Gabe pivoted, but said nothing, just started walking toward the path through the rain-forest exhibit.

But Marcel wasn't ready to let him go. "I'd be careful if I were you, Gabriel," he called, and the way he enunciated Gabe's name, the way a parent might speak to an errant child, made Evangeline's skin crawl.

Gabriel Fontenot was no child.

"Boys who play games—" he warned.

Gabe stopped, turned. "I'll make note of that," he said without one trace of the venom Evangeline knew he felt. "But you know what they say about people who've already lost everything."

Marcel picked up a champagne glass from the railing and lifted it toward Gabe. "You really think you've lost *everything*, Gabriel?"

It shouldn't have been possible for Gabe to look lethal, not while he wore an expensively cut tuxedo, with the breeze ruffling his burned-coffee hair and his lips curved into a smile. Maybe it was the whiskers shadowing his jaw. Or maybe it was the other shadow, the one that fell between the two men, of another man, a third man. Not Detective John D'Ambrosia, but Gabe's father, who remained there, positioned between the man who might have taken his life and the son who'd vowed to avenge him.

"I wasn't talking about myself," Gabe said in a chillingly soft voice. Then he strode from the patio. Saura and her detective fiancé shot a hard look at Evangeline, then Marcel, before they, too, slipped into the shadows, without ever having said a word.

Sometimes, Evangeline knew, words were not necessary.

But sometimes they were. *A good man,* she wished she'd been able to say. *An honest man. A man of deep integrity. A man who's loved and lost, who's been betrayed. A man who grew up too hard and too fast, who took on responsibility when he should have been flirting with irresponsibility. A man who—*

God help her, a man she wanted. Even now, even still.

"Well, that was certainly interesting," Marcel mused, strolling toward her. He dropped his cigarette but did not crush it out. Nearing her, he offered her the champagne. "Have you tried the shrimp remoulade yet? I really think you'll enjoy it."

Evangeline wasn't sure she'd ever wanted more to wipe

a smarmy smile off someone's face. "I'll keep that in mind," she said, but did not take the glass from his hands.

"You do that." He set the champagne on the railing, then reached inside his jacket and withdrew an an-tique silver case, tapped out another cigarette. "I have a few things to keep in mind, myself." And then he was gone.

Evangeline crossed to the railing and looked out over the river. To the south, a barge worked its way beneath the twin-span bridge that connected the Crescent City to its neighbor, Slidell. Both had been decimated by Katrina's floodwaters. Both had sat in ruin and squalor. But now both were on the mend, hope taking root where once there'd been only despair.

With the breeze whispering around her, she ran her finger along her bottom lip.

She heard the footsteps too late. Throat tight, she started to turn, but he was on her before she could move, crowding her with his body. Something rough and dark and rancid smelling came down over her head, bringing with it a cloying darkness.

"Scream," the low voice growled in her ear, "and it will be the last mistake you make."

Evangeline didn't come back. Gabe knew better than to watch, knew there was no longer a reason to stand vigil beside the eerily lit aquarium that doubled as a wall. He'd accomplished what he'd come to do. He'd baited the trap, watched Lambert come sniffing around. He'd played the game and hidden his cards. He'd pre-tended to be beaten. He'd pretended to be down.

The lure was sweet: for years Lambert had hungered for the legendary stained glass that had vanished during the Civil War. Museums in France wanted it back. They were willing to pay.

And Lambert…Lambert was willing to kill. Once he caught wind of the rumors Gabe had sent rippling through the city, that Gabe had located the object of his own father's obsession, Lambert would not be able to resist. He'd come sniffing around. But this time it would be Gabe standing in his way and, unlike his father, Gabe was prepared. The trap would spring, and Lambert would be the one caught.

And then Gabe could go on. And his need for Evangeline would be over.

Twenty minutes. That's how long had passed since Lambert had strolled back into the main lobby, with a cigarette in his hand and a self-satisfied smile on his face. He'd gone straight for his wife and slid his arm around her waist, posed for yet another picture.

But Evangeline…

Swearing softly, Gabe abandoned the feeding frenzy inside the saltwater tank and strode toward the rainforest exhibit. "Gabe, what's going on?" Jack asked into the earpiece.

"Nothing." He refused to run. *To her.*

But, God, his heart pumped with a violence that stunned. She was a grown woman, he knew that. She could come and go as she pleased. He knew that, too—she'd made sure that he did. She made her own choices, her own bed. If she'd chosen to ally herself with Marcel Lambert…

The cool breeze rushed him the second he emerged onto the patio. "Evangeline!" Her name practically ripped from his throat.

Stopping abruptly, he spun, found nothing. Not her, not anyone else. Just the circle of quietly swaying tiki torches and an orgy of shadows, a few ships on the river and the lingering scent of powder and vanilla.

"Gabe, maybe I should stay—"

"No."

"I can help you go through pictures, see what else we can find out about Darci. Friends maybe—"

"No."

"I'll fix sandwiches, then," Saura said, pivoting from the pile of folders and yearbooks she'd scouted out that afternoon. She and D'Ambrosia had dropped them by after leaving the fund-raiser.

"When was the last time you ate?" she pressed, as she always did. Somewhere along the line the rebellious cousin of his youth had taken on the role of mother hen.

He watched her glide toward his kitchen, looking sleek and elegant and impossibly refined in a swingy little bronze dress and high heels, her hair in a long elegant braid down her back, but saw only the girl she'd been, in her ratty cutoff shorts and flip-flops, her hair in pigtails and mud smeared on her face, wading through a creek bed in search of crawdads. Wherever Saura had been, Camille had been two steps behind….

"Not hungry," he said, intercepting her before she reached the kitchen. He'd been in there when the doorbell rang shortly before eleven. He'd had his hand on the bottle on the counter. He'd been at the door in a heartbeat, yanking it open—

"I had some of Lambert's jambalaya," he said with a dry little smile. "Kind of overdone, if you ask me."

She twisted toward him, nearly leveled him with the dark glow in her eyes. "It's going to happen, isn't it? After all this time…Marcel is going down."

He reached for his cousin's braid, as he had so many times over the years, and gave a soft tug. "In spades."

"What about Evangeline?" she asked, and his fingers stilled. "Where does she fit in? We tried to keep her inside, but—"

"Saura."

The transformation was immediate. She stopped and looked toward her fiancé, her eyes widening the way they had when she'd been a kid and Cain had busted her rifling through his albums.

And for a moment there, Gabe forgot about the cold fist twisting through him and the question about Lambert he refused to answer, the way Evangeline had looked in those tenuous moments before the black and the white had shattered into a thousand shades of gray.

There was only his headstrong cousin stopped in her tracks, the way D'Ambrosia looked as if he didn't know whether to turn her over his knee or kiss her senseless, and a realization that sliced to the bone. Neither wavered. But with a simple word, a look, either could bring the other to their knees.

D'Ambrosia's eyes literally gleamed. "You promised you wouldn't—"

"Just leave Evangeline to me," Gabe cut in before John could finish reminding her she wasn't supposed to nag and worry. "I've got her right where I want her."

Evangeline ripped the scratchy bag from her face and gulped in cool air. Her lungs screamed and her heart pounded, but she didn't let herself move, not until she was sure the man was gone.

They'd driven…she didn't know how long they'd driven. Or how far. There'd only been darkness and the monotone voice droning from the stereo. Once, she'd made a move for the door, but another voice had stopped her.

Don't make a mistake your brother will regret.

Now she blinked against the grittiness of her eyes and tried to orient herself. Her body protested, but she pulled herself upright and blinked again, stared between the bucket seats—to the familiar knobs of the radio.

Jimmy's car. She was in Jimmy's car…had been all along. It was her keys dangling from the ignition. Her purse sitting on the passenger seat as if no one else had been there, no one had dragged her from the fund-raiser and shoved her into the backseat, no one had driven for hours while—

She lifted her hands, saw only a hint of red circling her wrists, where the rope had been. Lunging between the seats, she grabbed her wrap and shoved her hand into the flimsy fabric before hitting the stereo's Eject button.

The cassette that had played over and over, while she'd been driven around town was no longer there.

Barely recognizing the strangled sound that broke from her throat, she reached for the purse—and saw the picture.

Jimmy. He lay on a small cot. A sheet covered his body, but not his bruised arms—and not his bruised face. His left eye was swollen shut. Blood leaked from beneath his right eye. His nose was…crooked, his lips busted.

Beside him sat a newspaper. Blinking against the rush of moisture, she looked at the headlines—and saw a picture of Marcel Lambert. The print was too small to read, but she didn't need to. She'd read it that morning. The article gushed about the fund-raiser, how Marcel was working to bring life back to the city, even when his own future hung in doubt, as if he were some kind of misunderstood, self-sacrificing hero.

She sat there so very still, staring at her brother and knowing, knowing without doubt, that he'd been hurt because of her. She'd been to the prison just that morning. But she'd been denied access. They'd told her he'd refused to see her. But now she knew. And now she wanted to throw up.

Numbly, she flipped the photo over and saw the words, the same words that had droned from the stereo in that mechanical voice, as she'd lain in the backseat,

Guilt and innocence…
It's never that black or white.
You have the power. You have the choice.
If Fontenot doesn't back off…he won't be the only one to suffer.

Jimmy would suffer. *Because of her.*

Her eyes filled, but Evangeline would not let the tears fall. Because she refused to buckle, refused to run and hide. Blinking, she looked up from the carefully printed words and stared out the window. And for the first time saw the houses. Quaint, tidy, well manicured. On each side of the tree-lined street. Adrenaline surged as she twisted toward the right and saw the soft glow from inside a small window. And the wide, screened-in porch. And the dark, slumbering trees.

Gabe…

It hurt to move. It hurt to breathe. But she could no more have stayed in Jimmy's car than she could have made her heart stop pounding.

What kind of man do you think I am?

The question taunted as she slid the picture into her purse and stepped into the cool breath of the night.

Numbly, almost robotically, she twisted back toward the car and reached for an old denim jacket on the floor behind the driver's seat, slipped it on. Then she quietly closed the door and crossed the street, walked toward the house.

Toward Gabe—and a choice she could no longer avoid.

Once he might have opened the door with one of those slow easy smiles she had so categorically not expected. In the weeks and months leading up to her arrival in New Orleans, she'd prepared herself for every contingency she'd been able to come up with. To hate him, to toy with him, to battle him. To bring him down.

But she had not prepared herself for those smiles that reached inside her.

And she'd not prepared herself for wanting, so damn bad, to find innocence, instead of guilt.

And she'd not prepared herself to feel anything other than hate. Certainly not compassion. And never, ever remorse.

To the soundtrack of cicadas and crickets, she stepped onto the porch and crossed to the screen door. But she did not open it. Instead, she lifted her hand and knocked.

With the first case she'd prosecuted, the jury had stayed out for eight days and two hours. She'd had to teach herself the art of patience, how to stay calm while each minute, each hour—*each day*—dragged by. To not let her imagination run away with her—and to not let her body betray her. Deliberations were never easy, even the short ones. Once, the jury had taken less than twenty minutes. The longest she'd had to wait—

There were no footsteps, no small window by the door to warn of his approach. Just the quiet click of the dead bolt. "What's the matter," he drawled. "Couldn't stay away—"

Twelve years. That was the longest she'd waited.

But then the hard wood door opened and he was there, and in that dark, deep place inside, she knew twelve years had been nowhere near long enough.

Chapter 11

He stood in the dim lighting of the entryway, with a thick white towel around his neck and jeans low on hips, his feet bare. His hair was damp, curling at the nape, but whiskers still covered his jaw. And in his eyes gleamed a dark light that made Evangeline want to step back, even as she wanted to step closer.

"Gabe." Her throat tightened around his name, but he gave no reaction, just stood there looking at her as if her mere presence were some kind of desecration.

The urge to yank open the screen door and go to him, to step into his arms and hold on, just hold on, pushed through her with a viciousness that stunned.

"We need to talk." She managed the words with the cool efficiency of an opening argument, as if it wasn't almost midnight and he hadn't turned his back on her. "About the case."

Shifting, he brought his shoulder up against the door frame. But somehow, he didn't lean. It was more as if he supported—everything. "Is that a fact?"

"Gabe, listen—"

"No, you listen, because I'm only going to say this once."

Her heart kicked hard as his eyes went even darker.

"You need to leave, Evangeline." Not *Evie*. Not even *catin*. But her full name, *Evangeline*, spoken as a judge might, with no trace of familiarity. "You need to turn around right now and walk away from here."

From him.

"That's not what I need," she whispered.

"The hell it's not." With the words a hard, strangled sound broke from his throat. "This is the last place you should be tonight."

But it was the only place she wanted to be—*and the only place someone else wanted her to be.* Beneath the denim of her jacket her wrists burned and she could again feel the rope that had bound her hands. Gone now. As if it had never even been there.

"Why not?" She kept the emotion from tearing through her voice. "You might try to punish me again?"

It was more a reckless taunt than a question. "This has nothing to do with punishment."

Maybe it was his voice, the absolute lack of emotion in it. Or maybe it was the way he looked at her, as if he felt…absolutely nothing. As if he didn't even know her. Didn't care.

Or maybe it was the way he dominated the doorway as unyieldingly as he dominated a courtroom. He'd made no move to open the screen door, no move to invite her in from the night.

Maybe it was all of that. Or none of it. But before she could remind herself of even one reason why she shouldn't move, she reached for the screen door and yanked it open, stepped inside.

Warmth was her first thought. Then…coffee.

"Doesn't it?" she whispered. And then she stepped into him, the way she should have done the night before. The way she'd wanted to do. Instead, she'd ripped away and forced herself to consider the fire and the evidence and the logical conclusion that a man who would stop at nothing to make sure he got what he wanted wouldn't think twice about destroying a little evidence.

She'd grabbed on to that thought, commanded herself to hold on to it, to use it to drive away the other thoughts that kept growing stronger in spite of everything she'd learned. The thoughts that wanted to erase twelve years of animosity and replace them with the gossamer fine hope that Gabriel Fontenot was not the ruthless, driven man she'd so desperately wanted him to be. Because she had the evidence that could make him fall. And if he fell, Jimmy could be free again, he could get his life back and his future.

But if Gabe wasn't that man…

It was a broken sound that slipped from her throat as she approached him, as his eyes darkened in those few seconds before she pushed up on her toes and pressed her mouth to his. Sliding her arms around his shoulders, she dug her fingers into his back and held on and kissed him.

His body was warm and solid and, as she dragged a hand around to the side of his face, the ache spread from her chest into her blood. He just stood there. He didn't lift a hand to her body, not to hold her, not to push her away. He didn't move his mouth, not to curse her or kiss her.

And, in that moment, the evidence fell around her in sharp dark sheets, driving home what she'd suspected from the moment he'd put his mouth to hers at the fund-raiser.

She jerked away and stepped back, forcing herself to breathe. "What's the matter?" she demanded with a flatness that masked the hurt. "Not as much fun without witnesses?"

Without Marcel Lambert there to see.

The house was dimly lit, the porch light off. Not far from where he stood the hardwood floor of the narrow entryway spilled into a large room. She could see the back of a sofa, a small television set, a fireplace and an almost-empty mantel. Off to the right was a kitchen, separated from the main room by a black granite counter-bar.

On it sat a bottle.

It shouldn't have been possible for the shadows to deepen, but somehow they did.

Before he could stop her—*before she could stop herself*—she shoved by him and crossed to the small kitchen. Beyond the pass-through, a single light shone on an old pine table, illuminating stacks of files and newspaper clippings, a few books—and an empty tumbler.

But it was the bottle of whiskey she grabbed.

"Is this why you want me to leave so bad?" she asked, holding it up toward the light.

Only a few drops remained.

"Put it down." Gabe's voice came from behind her, soft and controlled and one hundred percent lethal.

She spun toward him. "What were you trying to

prove?" But the answer came with the question, the faint residue of whiskey mingling with the coffee brewing. "Tonight. At the fund-raiser. Letting Lambert see us like that…"

Gabe closed in on her, his gaze dropping from her face along her body, slowly, meticulously, lingering on the bulky denim jacket that covered her dress—and concealed the bruises braceleting her wrists. Then just as slowly he lifted his eyes to hers. "Maybe I wasn't trying to prove anything."

Her hand tightened around the bottle. "Maybe," she conceded, even though she knew better. "But not likely. Not with you." He was always thinking, planning, always three steps ahead. "You always have an endgame."

The light in his eyes went out. "Not everything is a game, *catin.*"

The endearment did cruel, cruel things to her heart. It slammed against her ribs, for one dangerous moment cutting off everything else.

Not everything is a game.

But *this* was, she knew. *They* were. It was a game she had begun, an ill-fated house of cards she'd started to deal long before they'd even met. A game she alone could end, but both of them would lose. She'd gone after him with a single-mindedness that had consumed her. Playing him, offering him the illusion of friendship but yanking it back when the situation stopped being so crystal clear, never stopping to think about what she was doing to him.

Now she stood in his empty little kitchen in his empty little house, square and center between him and the man who'd made his mother a widow and a young boy grow up hideously fast.

Before Gabe could bring Lambert down, he had to get through her, the woman who'd fed him false information and set him up, waited to see him fall. Once again his fate rested in her hands.

That's why he'd kissed her. Not because she'd slipped into his blood, but to make sure she never did.

"Gabe." His name was barely more than a rasp. "This has to stop." With one last glance at the empty bottle, she returned it to the counter, next to a green apple and a neat stack of mail. "I know you want to bring down Lambert, but playing vigilante isn't the way to do it. He knows—"

If Fontenot doesn't back off, he won't be the only one to suffer....

"Of course he knows," Gabe said. "That's never been a secret."

No, the secrets were hers. And before all was said and done, they would destroy everything. He would hate her, but if she could make him back off Lambert, at least Gabe would be alive.

"By dragging me into your game—" she started to say, but Gabe chose that moment to come to life.

He stepped toward her and bracketed his hands against the counter on either side, shredded her with one of those slow, easy smiles. "I don't recall any dragging."

Her heart strummed low and hard and deep. He stood so close she could feel him, all of the heat and the strength and the contempt. But there was something else, too, a struggle that disturbed, even as it fascinated.

He was right. No one had dragged her. She alone had charged into his life. She alone had gone after him.

Throat tight, she lifted her chin, keeping her attorney's face in place and refusing to fall for his blatant attempt to use sexual innuendo to misdirect. That he would touch her now—

She should have been angry. And maybe she was. But something else whispered through her, something warm and fragile and so completely wrong….

"It could result in a mistrial." She had to force the words out, even though they were true. "Lambert's attorneys could use that little kiss at just the right moment, paint me to be every bit as biased as you are."

Unless the D.A. removed her from the case.

Gabe's eyes took on a lethal glow. "There's no such thing as bias when it comes to murder."

"But there is when it comes to the judicial system," she threw back. "I get it, Gabe. Okay? I get it. I know you want Lambert. I know you want to make him pay, see him fall. But playing games with me isn't the way."

"You sure about that?" He stroked a finger along her cheekbone. "Is that why you came here in the middle of the night, Evangeline? To teach me Law 101?"

Push away. She knew that's what she should do. She knew that, just as she knew so much else. But that dark rhythm wouldn't stop singing through her. "I came to tell you to back off."

He claimed to want nothing to do with her, but he kept right on touching her, sliding his finger down to her jawbone. "Did you now?"

She knew she had to breathe, but with each breath, all she did was draw the scent of him—of soap and coffee and man—deep inside. "Arceneaux wants answers. He wants to know what happened last night—"

"And what did you tell him?" The question was soft, the way he spoke to a defendant just before he broke them into a thousand pieces. "That you were asleep?

That you woke up and found me gone? That within seconds the whole place went up—"

And it all would have been true. "It would be your
word against mine, wouldn't it?" she pointed out, refusing to be backed into a corner, even if somehow she
had let him box her in.

"You didn't tell him anything."

Her heart kicked hard. With a determination that
came from all those years she'd pursued a single goal,
she grabbed his wrist and pulled his hand from her face,
twisted from his arms. "Not yet."

And again, the light in Gabe's eyes dimmed. "Go
home, Evangeline. It's late—"

"You'd like that, wouldn't you?" she said, backing
deeper into his house. "You'd like me to roll over and
play dead, so you can keep bulldozing your way through
this case. Don't you get it?" she asked, trying to ignore
the play of shadows against the lines of his face and the
stupid white towel draped around his neck, the swirl of
dark hair trailing down from his navel.

"You can't just make up the rules as you go
along—" Even if that's exactly what she'd done.

She broke toward the table before he could stop her,
looking for the proof she needed—the proof she had no
doubt she would find.

Yearbooks, she recognized instantly. Three of them
in a neat little stack, the one on top open to a page with
rows of class pictures.

But it was the open folder that stopped her, the me-
ticulous drawing of an orgy of angels and demons, a
stack of handwritten notes…and an old black-and-white
photograph. "My God," she whispered, reaching for the
worn image. "Lambert…"

She felt Gabe move, felt him crowd in behind her.

"I thought they were just rumors," she said. "People with nothing better to talk about…" But now she saw, and she knew. The picture was old and torn and faded—of four young men, happy and relaxed, on what looked to be a fishing trip somewhere in a marsh. Marcel Lambert had changed little in what had to be at least twenty-five years, nor had his brother, Nathan, who'd been killed only a month before. The third man was cut off, only his legs visible. But the fourth…

She twisted toward Gabe, her chest aching at the realization that every morning when he looked in the mirror, it was his father he saw staring back at him.

All her life she'd heard about the stained glass smuggled out of France during the Revolution. She'd heard of its mysterious healing powers and the bloodshed that followed in its wake. She'd heard about the Yankee soldiers during the Civil War who'd sought to capture it—and the young woman who'd buried it somewhere in the swamp before she'd been apprehended. She'd committed suicide while in captivity….

But the stories weren't just confined to her childhood. She'd heard the whispers tonight, at the fundraiser. She'd heard the idle talk that the stained glass had been found….

The pieces all fell together, not just from tonight but across months and years, creating a truth that sobered. She twisted toward Gabe, found the oddest expression on his face. "You're laying a trap, aren't you?" Technically it was a question. But she didn't need the answer.

That's why he was so calm. That's why he was so controlled. He knew exactly what he was doing. That's why he watched her through those narrow, assessing eyes.

He removed the photograph from her hands. "You should go, Evangeline."

Her mind worked fast, knitting the evidence together. "So what…you make Marcel think you found what he and your father were looking for? Then what, Gabe? Then what? You set yourself up as bait?" The thought sickened. "You wait and see if he tries to kill you for it?"

The way he'd killed Gabe's father.

Gabe didn't so much as flinch. "If that's what it takes."

"No." It was more a horrified breath than a word. "I'm not going to let you do that."

But his eyes only hardened. "You can't stop me."

Reckless adrenaline crashed through her.

Gabe was wrong. She could stop him. With those few words to the D.A. They would be a lie, but they would keep Gabe alive. He would hate her…but he was going to hate her, anyway.

There was nothing else to say, not between them. Only a phone call to make. It was what she'd wanted all along, to see Gabe fall. But not like this. *And not anymore.*

"I was wrong in coming here," she said, carefully measuring her words. Gabe was an excellent game player, a master of the bluff. That he'd let her see his notes could be no accident. She turned to leave, but his hand caught her wrist before she could take so much as a step.

She tried to hide the wince. She tried to keep her expression blank. But the pain seared clear to the bone. She stopped and drew into herself, recovered quickly.

But Gabe had already seen.

* * *

Gabe knew violence. He'd seen it and witnessed it—the sheet covering his father's body, the ugly yellow tape streaking across the study, the lingering scent of cleaning chemicals. He'd been there when Val had died. And the girl in Florida. He'd read the police report. He knew the details.

He knew violence. He'd prosecuted violence. He'd convicted violence. It was nothing new to him.

But the greenish smears circling Evangeline's wrists stopped him.

"Who did this to you?" he asked with brutal stillness, because if he let go, for even one little breath…

He didn't know. Didn't know what would happen if he let go.

She tried to jerk her arm out of his grip. "Let go of me!"

He loosened his grip, but didn't release her. Didn't release himself. "Who did this to you, damn it?"

Evangeline glared at him, and, for the first time since she'd arrived, he saw it in her eyes, the stark, dark glow. *The fear.* "It was crowded at the benefit—" she tried, but the tightness just kept right on twisting.

"Don't lie to me!" Someone had done this to her. While he'd been so blinded by his need to test, to punish, someone had hurt her. "That's why you're here, isn't it?" Why she hadn't returned to the aquarium after he'd let anger drive him, after he'd pulled her into his arms and used her just as she'd used him.

"That's why you're threatening me to back off," he realized, just as he realized an equally sobering truth. Evangeline hadn't known Gabe when she set him up… but he had known her. Known and wanted.

But he'd hung her out to dry, anyway. Had even let her see his file on Marcel Lambert, just to gauge what she already knew—and what she'd do with any new information. "Someone threatened you—"

The dark hair falling into her face was no longer glossy as it had been at the aquarium. He should have noticed that, damn it, when he'd first opened the door, expecting Saura, but finding her. He should have noticed that and so many other little telltale signs.

But he'd been too busy seeing her through his own distorted lens.

"No," she said with a firmness that ground through him.

"Yes." Because of him. Because he'd dragged her into his game. "Someone threatened you," he said again. "Someone scared you."

The light in her eyes deepened. "I know what I'm doing."

"Tell me, then," he said, but couldn't stop touching her. Wasn't about to let her go. "Tell me what you're doing."

She swiped the hair from her face, drawing his attention to the dryness of her lips. "I'm trying to protect an innocent man."

"By letting a guilty man go free?" The question was quiet. The roar inside was not.

This time when she tugged, he let go, and she stepped back. "Is that what you think of me? That I would sell out like that?"

What kind of man do you think I am?

The question, the memory, scraped.

"I was scared, Gabe," she said, and her voice broke. "Is that what you want to hear?" She brought her hand to her wrist and gently covered the bruises. "I was on the patio after you and Marcel left. I...never heard him approach."

Something hard and dark twisted through Gabe. "You weren't there when I went back."

The quick flare of her eyes, the surprise and the hope and the devastation, punished. But she shook her head as if to send it away, to deny. "He put a bag over my head," she said, and the sickness spread deeper. "We drove...for a long time."

While Gabe had been savoring the trap he'd laid.

"There was some kind of voice," she said, and, at last, the edges of the gutsy attorney frayed, giving him a glimpse of the woman inside, the woman who'd been terrorized and threatened, but who'd refused to break, to crumble. Who'd come to him...

"And then he stopped," she said. "And everything got quiet. It was a few minutes before I realized he was gone and not coming back...before I realized where I was."

Gabe didn't let himself move, because with brutal certainty he finally knew. He knew what would happen if he let go. He would drag her into his arms and hold her, hold her tight...the way she refused to admit that she needed. "Where were you?"

Something about her changed. Her expression, maybe. Her body language. It all seemed to soften and, when she lifted her eyes, the rip of awareness cut clean through him. "Here."

It was not the answer he'd expected. "The person who attacked you drove you here?"

"Yes."

He looked at her standing there, the odd light in her

eyes and the tangled hair falling against the fading
bruise. In the courtroom she looked tough and invincible. But here, now, she looked small and vulnerable
in ways he'd never expected.

"So you could come inside and do his bidding…" he
realized. Just as she'd done.

Again she lifted a hand to swipe the hair from her
face. But this time she stepped toward him, rather than
away. "That's not why I came to you."

He didn't trust himself to move. Because then he
might touch. And if he touched— "No?"

"*No.*" Then the gutsy attorney was back and she
did what he'd refused to do, destroyed the distance between them and pushed up on her toes. "This is why,"
she whispered, and her mouth brushed his.

Earlier he'd simply stood still. Earlier, when she'd
first arrived, he'd stood like a complete ass, blinded by
the need for revenge that had driven him for years, never
realizing it had distorted everything. For so long there'd
been only the black and the white. He'd never realized
that when they collided, there would be gray.

"The whole time we drove around," she murmured
against his mouth, "all I could think was Gabe…God,
Gabe…"

He didn't let himself move.

"You have every right to hate me after what I did last
fall," she said, resting a hand against the side of his
face. He couldn't stop the wince, but she laid her palm
there, anyway, kept her eyes on his. "To push me away.
I lied to you. I pretended I was your friend, that you
could trust me."

The raw honesty shredded. "Damn it, Evie…"

"But I didn't know." She kept right on talking. "It

doesn't excuse anything, but I didn't know you... didn't know what kind of man you are. The evidence looked bad—"

"And evidence never lies." He bit the words out. It was the ultimate irony for an attorney.

"But it does! I know that now. Sometimes things aren't what they seem. Sometimes you have to dig deeper to see the truth."

He looked down at her face, only a breath from his, and finally he saw. The truth. She'd showed up on his doorstep in the middle of the night, looking beautiful despite the shadows in her eyes. She'd risked everything to come to him, but like a coward, he'd just stood there while she stepped inside his house and put her mouth to his, despite the fact she'd been ordered to drive a knife into his back.

She'd risked everything...and he'd given nothing.

"You *could* have started that fire," she said, still talking quietly, gently. And slowly she lifted her other arm, this time curving it around his rib cage, to feather her hand along his back. "But you didn't," she said, and the words fed that dark place inside him. Fed and destroyed. "I know that now...knew it last night," she added. Abruptly, she pulled her hand from his face and grabbed for his hand, dragged it to her chest. "I knew that here," she said, pressing his palm against her jacket.

He didn't stop his fingers from flattening.

"But I was trying to think like an attorney," she said. "Not a woman. I was trying to make myself consider all the possibilities and not be blinded by what I wanted—"

Through the soft denim, he felt the frenetic riff of her heart and knew he couldn't just stand there much longer. "What *do* you want, Evangeline?"

The light in her eyes dimmed. But it was her soft smile that damn near sent him to his knees. "I'd heard about you before I came to New Orleans," she said. "Gabriel Fontenot, son of the South. Invincible prosecutor. My professors talked about you. We studied your casework, your style. I knew about your family," she added. "Your reputation, how well you could bluff. And maybe I built you up in my mind, turned you into some demigod who couldn't be touched, didn't want to be touched."

Except now she was touching him. And God help him, he was touching her. Touching Evangeline. The way he'd wanted to do for so freaking long.

"You were with Val," she whispered, looking away from him briefly, toward the nearly empty house. After Val's death, he'd gotten rid of everything she'd brought into his life.

Everything but the shadows inside of him and the inability to trust. Not just others. But himself.

"Everyone said you'd been together forever," Evangeline was saying, "that you would get married. And I respected that. But then the D.A. asked me to engage you on a personal level—"

"To feed me dirty information." For the first time he allowed himself to see it through her eyes, the young new prosecutor being assigned to a special task force by her boss, the man many believed would be the next lieutenant governor. She hadn't known Gabe, only the rumors.

And the rumors about the Robichaud family were anything but good. At the time many had believed his cousin Cain guilty of murder. And that Gabe had pulled strings to avoid an indictment. Further back than that, the scandal with his father's alleged suicide...

"Yes. To feed you dirty information. But somewhere

along the line everything blurred and I saw something in your eyes…and I—I didn't want it to be a game anymore." She returned her hand to the side of his face, whisper soft. "The first time you kissed me—"

He'd thought his friend was dead. They'd buried him that day. The memory of the explosion had echoed in Gabe's ears while Alec's widow had tried to comfort him. Sweet God, Tara was the one who'd lost any chance of reconciling with her estranged husband, but *she'd* tried to comfort *Gabe*. But the devastation in her eyes—

He should have gone home to Val. That would have been the logical thing to do. But Gabe had gone to his office instead. It wasn't until Evangeline had walked in that he understood why. He'd warned her to leave….

"It made me sick to feed you the false leads," she said, exploring his face with her fingers. "After I did, I went into the ladies' room and threw up."

He closed his eyes, didn't want to see.

"And then the truth came out…" She kept on, with her words and her fingers, the press of her body, the unforgiving scent of powder and vanilla. "When I heard about Val—" her voice broke "—the lie she'd been living, and I knew I was just one more knife in your back…."

It all closed in on him, the lies and the deception, the games, the truth, and he knew if he stayed there one second longer, with her hands on his body and her mouth only a breath away, the ironclad control he'd been holding in a death grip would crumble and she would be the only one in its path. He would take then, take what he'd wanted, needed, for too damn long.

Instead, he ripped away and strode from her, from the table full of lies and revenge and hatred. He stopped at the window, intending to look out into the darkness.

But saw only the soft glow of Evangeline's reflection.

"Last night you asked me what kind of man I thought you were."

The burn started low and spread fast. He refused to move, though, couldn't look away. Not from her, from Evangeline, walking so steadily toward him. The window gave him every detail, the glow of vulnerability in her eyes and the stubborn set of her chin, the swing of her tangled hair and the denim jacket hanging open to reveal her little black dress.

"You're a good man," she said, and the soft words serrated with a viciousness that almost had him putting a fist through the window.

He'd used her. He'd openly and deliberately used her to further his revenge against Marcel Lambert. And then when he was done with her, when she'd served her purpose, he'd not only discarded her, but had thrown her to the wolves.

"An honorable one," she whispered, refusing to stop, despite the rigid way he stood. "Loyal."

He could see more than just her steady progress through the reflection. He could see himself, the uncompromising stance of his body.

"You do the right thing for the right reasons." With those words she closed the last of the distance between them. "You stand up for what you believe in. You care and you hurt."

Her hand skimmed his shoulder. It should have been cool. There was no reason for warmth. But it was warmth that seeped through him.

And it was warmth that destroyed.

"I saw you the night you buried Alec—"

He twisted toward her so fast she had no chance to

prepare. "Don't," he snapped, but she didn't back away and she didn't stop.

"And I've seen you with your family, your friends. With Jack last night, the way you dragged him from the fire…" Her eyes almost seemed to glow. "And me," she whispered. "At the warehouse."

The memory sliced back, the vicious moment he'd seen her sprawled beneath him on the dirty floor. "I hurt you."

"But you didn't mean to," she countered, keeping her eyes steady on his. "You didn't want to." Almost hesitantly, she moistened her lips. "Don't you think I know that, Gabe? Don't you think I know that you've been spinning for months now, trying to get a footing? To get back to the man you are?" Sliding her hand into his hair, she left only her thumb against the side of his face. "The man who tackled me, who taunted me, who kissed me at the fund-raiser…that's not you."

He wanted to pull away. He needed to pull away, to quit looking into her eyes. Quit seeing. Quit believing.

Quit wanting.

"Yes—" he gritted the words out "—it is."

Very little light made it to the back of the room, leaving only shadows to play against her face. "Everyone has a breaking point," she whispered, and his chest wound even tighter.

Nothing prepared him for her to feather her mouth against his. Or for her words, dark, drugging. Broken. "And I've hit mine."

He'd discovered Evangeline's duplicity late one afternoon in November. The next day Val had died in his arms, and he'd realized everything he'd believed about her, the life they'd been building, had been a lie. He didn't remember much after that, days, weeks, they all rolled together.

"You asked what I want," Evangeline whispered with another little kiss to his mouth. "The answer is you."

She was so soft. And sweet. Warm. He'd told himself it was all an illusion, part of the game the D.A. had asked her to play, but here, now, like this, there were no games, no agendas.

"And I have for so long."

Just her. Evangeline. The woman he'd tried to carve out of his life, but who'd refused to go away, even when she should have. She'd come to him, the way she had so many other nights, when he'd found her in the darkness of his dreams.

"A few days before Christmas I woke up in my car," he stunned himself by saying. "It was overcast." Gray everywhere. "Cold." His engine had been running. "And I didn't know where I was—" he hesitated, gave her a moment to absorb what he was saying "—or how I got there."

Her eyes went dark. "You don't have to do this—"

"My mouth was dry." Like cotton. And he'd smelled stale bourbon on his clothes.

She said nothing at that, just kept watching, touching.

"I was by the lake," he told her.

Against the side of his face, her fingers tensed. "Alone?"

"An empty bottle of bourbon on the floor and pain pills in my lap." Val's semiautomatic on the passenger seat. But he didn't tell Evangeline that, didn't see any point. "I sat there a long time." Because for the first time in his life, he flat damn had not known where to go. He could have called Cain or Saura, Jack. He knew that. But he hadn't known how, hadn't wanted them to see him like that. "The sun was trying to break through the clouds…."

Briefly her eyes closed, then opened.

"It was almost eleven when I got home and brewed coffee, took a shower." He looked down at the dark hair falling into her face, but still, did not allow himself to touch. "Then I got a bottle of whiskey." He could still see the way the clerk had looked at him, the pity in her eyes. "And a refill on my prescription."

"No," she whispered, and then came her other hand, lifted to the other side of his face with a tenderness that should not have been possible, not between them.

"And I put them on the counter." Where he could see them every morning. "Everyone thought I was spinning out of control," he said. Saura and John…Cain. One by one they'd stop by his house, checking up on him. "But I never took one sip, one pill."

She slid her thumb toward his lower lip, where she rubbed.

"I just kept holding on," he muttered. "So goddamned tight, because I knew if I let go again, for even one minute—"

Something hard and dark flashed through her eyes. "Don't. Gabe. Don't tell me to leave—"

Slowly he lifted a hand to her face. "I wasn't going to." And slowly he touched. "But if you stay—"

"Let go," she said before he could finish. Then, softer, *"Let go…"*

The words slipped in through the shadows, and like a battered levee, the restraint he'd been exerting didn't just let go.

It broke.

Chapter 12

Evangeline knew the exact second Gabe let go.

For so long he'd been holding back from her, separate from her, as if an invisible wall had slammed down between them.

She should have stayed away from him. That would have been the logical thing to do. She should have been glad when he'd exposed her role in the D.A.'s sting and turned his back on her. She should have welcomed the reprieve.

But it had already been too late, she now knew. From the moment he'd tackled her in the warehouse, the wall she'd hammered between them had started to crumble. He'd formed an unholy alliance with her not because of any lingering desire to be with her, but because he'd needed her.

Needed. *Her.*

The words punished. He crushed her in his arms and his mouth came down against hers, as his whiskers scraped her jaw and his hands tangled into her hair, as the heat of his flesh seared through her clothes.

"Evangeline," he breathed as she opened to him, opened and gave and took. *"Evie."*

Everything fell away—the distant past and the recent past, plans and strategies and reality—and she reached for him, yanked the thick towel from around his shoulders and put her hands to the hard planes of his back, even as he shoved at the denim jacket.

"Let go," she said again, as her heart kept right on breaking. She'd never imagined—ever—how much he'd been holding back, how much control he'd been exerting to keep it all together.

To keep her away.

But she knew that now, felt it in the rough glide of his hands over her body and the greedy slant of his mouth. In his kiss she tasted a hunger that rocked her and a hurt that she wanted to chase away, the faint remains of coffee—but no whiskey. None, at all.

But I never took one sip, one pill.

He'd been testing himself, she realized. Not casually, as most people would do, but by putting temptation right in front of him. Every day. He'd tested himself and driven himself, isolated himself from everything and everyone who might have offered him an easy way out.

"You," he murmured against her mouth, and the rhythm of her heart changed. "You wouldn't go away," he said in a hoarse strangled voice. "Even when you should have."

"No," she whispered, loving the feel of him, all of him. Of Gabe. This was how she'd wanted him to come to her, with an unchained hunger that sang through her.

It had killed her to stand on the sidelines and watch his world blow up around him, to not be able to go to him or help him. To hold him or love—

Love.

The word should have stopped her. Instead, it drove her, and all she could think was more. *Now.*

"So beautiful," he muttered, sliding his mouth along her jaw to her neck. She heard the rasp break from her throat and arched into him, thrilling to the scrape of his whiskers against her neck. His hands moved restlessly along her back, as if he wanted to touch all of her at once. Take all of her.

More...

"Yes," she urged as he slid a hand around her rib cage to cup her breast, and the heat curled deeper. "Yes..." And then everything went blank and mindless and she wasn't sure who moved first, whether she dragged him or he dragged her; she only knew that his mouth returned to hers and the kiss deepened, even as they slammed into the closest wall.

"Yes," she said again, and all she could think was now, more. Closer. Everything.

So long. For so long she'd waited. And for so long she'd denied. She'd almost lost him in the process. And now—

She ran her hands along the planes of his body, loving the corded muscles of his back and the strength in his arms. Then the flatness of his stomach, down the dark trail of hair to the waistband of his jeans, where she fumbled with the snap and the zipper. The need to feel him drove her. All of him. To feel and hold and love—

But his hands were moving, too, restlessly, almost frenzied, shoving the denim jacket from her arms as his mouth left hers and slid to her collarbone, sprinkled little kisses along her shoulder.

Let go, she'd told him.

Let go, she'd told herself.

But she'd never imagined…only dreamed. And then he was there, hot and hard and heavy in her hand, and everything fell away, everything but the need. The need for him. For this man. For Gabe.

Gabe.

He hiked her leg up around his hip and she felt him start to move, start to lift her from her feet. But that wasn't what she wanted. She wanted here. She wanted now. Like this, with all the fire and passion and emotion boiling between them.

"No," she murmured, pushing at his jeans.

He pulled back and looked down at her, rocked her with the dark cobalt gleam in his eyes. "Evie—"

Her slow smile defied the frenetic rush of her breath. She kept her eyes on his and lowered her leg, made quick work of her panties. Then came his jeans, down his legs and kicked from his ankles. And then she reached for him, slid her arms around his shoulders as she returned her leg to his waist and felt him pressed up against her. "Let go," she murmured again.

Because she had. She'd let go. Of everything. Except Gabe. And the truth that rocked her world.

"This," he muttered, but she didn't know what he meant, didn't want words. Just him. She threaded a hand through his hair and urged him closer, couldn't stop the mewl that tore from her throat when his mouth slanted against hers as he braced her against the wall, curved one hand around her waist as his other slid between her legs and found her slick and ready.

Then he was there, Gabe, filling her, sliding deep. With a hoarse little moan she welcomed him, closing her eyes and arching into him as her bones threatened to melt. This, she realized as her body adjusted to the size of him. *This*. Him. "Gabe…"

He slid his mouth from hers and buried his face in her hair, started moving again, sliding out for one brief second before pushing back in. Again. And again. With each deep thrust her blood hummed and her body burned and she held him tighter, tighter. His skin was hot and slippery, and when he started to move faster, she knew she'd used her nails.

But then his mouth was on hers again, hers on his, claiming and seeking and wanting, needing, their bodies moving together with an abandon she'd never expected, giving and taking and…letting go, even as they clung to each other. Even as they held on.

"Gabe." Maybe she spoke. Maybe she didn't. There was no way to know, not when he rested his forehead to hers and drove in one last time, drove in hard and deep with a need that almost sent her to her knees.

Instead, she held on and simply shattered.

She still had her dress on. The slinky fabric prevented skin from touching skin, but did nothing to conceal the pounding of his heart. It slammed steadily against hers, as it had for the past…

Evangeline had no idea. No idea how much time had passed, how long they'd stood there in the shadows of his sparsely furnished living room. There was only the press of body to body, and the stillness and her dress bunched up between them.

She never would have imagined. She never *could*

have imagined. Gabe was a man of control and rigor and discipline. Even his slow easy smiles were deliberate, calculated. He always had an angle. Always had a strategy. He never let go, never lost control.

Opening her eyes, she looked up at him, felt everything inside her start to rush. With his dark hair falling against his forehead and the glow to his eyes, the whiskers shadowing his jaw and his chest bare, he looked as though he'd stepped straight out of her dreams. Except for the wince.

And it stripped her bare. He was the one who stood completely naked, she the one with her dress still on, but she'd never felt more exposed in her life. She opened her mouth, found only a whisper. "Hey."

The light in his eyes darkened. "Hey." It was only an echo of what she'd said, but his voice was rough and raw, tentative almost, unsure. Then came his hand, the single finger to the side of her mouth. "You okay?"

The tenderness in his voice, of the flesh beside her mouth, rocked her. But then she remembered the roughness of his whiskers, and she knew why he looked so horrified.

This time the tenderness was hers, starting in her chest and streaming through her, warming everywhere it touched. And because she couldn't stand it one second longer, couldn't just stand there and not touch him, when he'd touched her so deeply, she lifted a hand to his mouth and skimmed her thumb along his lower lip.

"Why wouldn't I be?" she murmured with a slow smile.

He didn't move; she wasn't sure he breathed. "You're still dressed."

And something inside her just melted. Gabe was one of those men who always knew what to do or say, how to handle a situation. Nothing rattled him. Nothing rocked him. But here, standing naked in the shadows of his living room, with his jeans in a heap on the floor, her panties tossed on top of them, with abrasions on her face and scratches along his back, he looked as if he didn't have a clue what to do.

Because she still had her dress on.

The dichotomy charmed. It wasn't fair to laugh. She knew that. But the look on his face, the hard line of his mouth and dark light to his eyes... Maybe it should have sobered her. Maybe it should have hurt or disappointed. But instead it endeared.

"Oops," she said, and felt her eyes go heavy. She stepped into him then and dragged her hand down to his chest, where she skimmed her thumb along the mauve of his flat nipple.

"I'm thinking maybe you should let go more often," she murmured, leaning in for a teasing kiss. He didn't move, not when she used her tongue, not when she pulled him into her mouth. "Gabe," she started, glancing up. But then she saw his face.

No one had ever looked at her that way, with a violent clash between need and restraint. No one had ever touched her while trying so very, very hard not to. No one had ever made her feel so very fragile, while at the same time so very, very strong.

This was the Gabe she knew, the Gabe she'd fallen in love with despite all the evidence she'd stacked against him. This was the Gabe who was in control and knew what he wanted, who went after it.

"Do you have any idea," he rasped, and finally he moved, finally he reached for her, returned his hands to her body, "any idea at all what you do to me?"

All her life she'd been a dreamer. And all her life she'd found them through sleep. But for the first time, the dream started while her eyes were open.

"Maybe," she said, and all those horrible shades of gray fell away, leaving only Gabe standing in stark relief. Gabe, whom she knew now; Gabe, whom she trusted.

Gabe, whom she wanted.

"But maybe you should show me," she whispered, curving her arms around his neck. He slid his arms lower then, used them to lift.

Holding on, she pressed into him and wrapped her legs around his waist. She'd always known he was strong, that beneath those tailored suits was the body of an athlete. But nothing prepared her for the reality of him, his muscular legs and flat stomach, his chest. Tilting her face up, she drank in the feel of him moving against her as he strode from the living room. Their mouths met and she opened to him, threaded a hand through his hair as the kiss deepened and he carried her into the darkness.

She slayed him.

Through the midnight quiet Gabe could hear Evangeline's breath, the rhythm of her heart. But she said nothing, not with words; asked no questions and made no demands, requested no promises. She just curved her legs around his waist and held on, kissed him as if she'd been waiting for him her whole life. He carried her through the shadows of the house he'd once shared with another woman, and finally he saw. Finally he knew.

She should have walked away. She should have stayed away. He'd given her every reason to. But she'd refused to turn her back on him, had kept vigil long after she should have given up.

But giving up was not an option. She was tough and gutsy and tenacious. She didn't scare, didn't run. Even when she should. Someone had threatened her tonight. Someone had gone to great lengths to bend her to their will. To break her. She'd come to Gabe as instructed, but that's where the compliance ended. She'd reached out when she should have pushed.

She'd given honesty when lies would have been safer.

She'd made him let go….

The master bedroom was the last door on the right, but he'd turned left, into the spare room. He'd purchased new furniture two months before, but he didn't want Evangeline to so much as think she was in Val's shadow. Because she wasn't. And never would be.

Evangeline had been the one casting a shadow, from the first day he'd seen her standing in the courthouse cafeteria.

"Evie." Moonlight streamed through the blinds and played against her face, making the sweep of her lashes against her cheeks look impossibly long—and the scrape next to her mouth impossibly heinous. Her eyes were closed. "Look at me."

He felt her tense, felt her breath feather against his chest and the muscles of her legs tighten. But for a long moment she did nothing, said nothing, and the frenzy of what he'd let happen in the living room twisted through him. He'd never taken a woman that way, never been so desperate to be inside that he hadn't even bothered to wait until she was undressed, had just pressed up against a wall and pushed inside—

The light in her eyes blanked the memory. It took a

second to register, the soft glow, the absolute lack of any recrimination whatsoever. Of just…contentment.

Maybe even amusement.

"You were so wrong," he muttered. "When you first joined the D.A.'s office and you turned and looked at me with that smile of yours—" with a single finger, he skimmed her bottom lip "—I knew I was in trouble."

A sweep of dark hair fell into her face, hiding the abrasion. But not the truth.

"I knew I should stay away from you, but everywhere I turned, you were there—"

Because she'd been deliberately infiltrating his life.

He didn't say the words, didn't need to. The shadow fell over her, anyway. "Gabe, don't—"

"You couldn't have done it." For months he'd condemned her, never connecting the dots to realize that if she was the perpetrator, that made him the victim.

Gabriel Fontenot was no one's victim.

"You couldn't have done what the D.A. asked you to do," he said, feathering his fingers out to her cheekbone, "if I hadn't let you." He'd fought it, tried to pretend he didn't walk into the courthouse each morning looking forward to seeing her, but now the truth bled through him. "If I'd been happy with Val, I wouldn't have even seen you, much less…"

It shouldn't have been possible for her to go more still. There in his arms, with her long legs curved around his waist, she barely breathed. "Much less, what?"

"Wanted you."

Her eyes flared, darkened, and his body started to harden all over again. "I tried to deny it," he said, because she deserved to know. "I'd made a commitment to Val and, even if things weren't great, I didn't know how to walk away from her." He'd tried. After the first year they'd broken up several times. Once, she'd called him to say goodbye.

He'd found her unconscious in her apartment, an empty bottle of sleeping pills beside her. "I thought she needed me."

At last, Evie moved. She brought a hand to his neck, trailing her fingertips along his throat. "But what did you need, Gabe?"

Maybe it was the softness of her voice. Or maybe it was the way she looked at him, the soul-bearing earnestness in her eyes. Maybe the feel of her wrapped around him—and the memory of being inside.

But the answer seared clear to the bone. "You," he said. *Her.*

The moonlight kept filtering in through the blinds, casting shadows across her face. "Gabe."

It was just his name, that was all she said. But there was an ache there, a pain, that shredded. He'd done this to her. He'd pushed her away, pushed hard.

Because he flat damn hadn't known how to do anything else.

"You'd made me feel things," he said. "Want things I'd forgotten existed. You'd made me feel alive." Vital. "You'd made me look forward to coming to the courthouse, to seeing you—"

Her hand fell away from his shoulder. "And then you found out about the I.A. investigation."

The words fell like bombs. "Yes." He wasn't sure who let go first. "Then I'd found out." If she pushed back, or if he released. He only knew her legs no longer curved around his waist, that she was standing there barefoot with her dress wrinkled, her chin at a fierce angle—like a heretic about to be stoned alive.

"Gabe." This time his name was barely a whisper. "I never expected—"

"Neither did I." The stoicism in her eyes ripped through him, the way she kept bracing herself for him to push her away.

"But I couldn't get you out of my blood," he said slowly, reaching for her as he did so. He curved his hands around her shoulders to the back of the dress, where he found the zipper. There, he tugged. "Couldn't forget the way you made me feel—want."

The shock in her eyes rocked him.

"That day I'd woken up by the lake," he said as the slinky fabric pooled at her feet, revealing the soft swell of her breasts, lower to the curve of her waist, her hips… "I'd picked up the phone and dialed a number."

She lifted her eyes to his.

"You," he said, returning his hands to her shoulders. "I'd called you." Because in the stillness of his empty little house, with his head pounding and his world tilting, he'd forgotten. He'd forgotten the dirty truths. Had forgotten about the night he'd confronted her in her office, when he'd wanted so damn bad for her to deny his accusations.

He'd forgotten, had only known that he'd craved her more than the whiskey and pain pills.

"Then I'd remembered," he said, "and hung up."

She kept her eyes on his, stepped closer. It started slow, the smile, a curve of her mouth more wistful than happy. "I would have come."

"I know." And he did. He'd known it then, too.

That was why he'd hung up. Because the black and

the white that had defined his life had merged into something dark and shadowy and dangerous. Evangeline would have come, but Gabe had no idea what he would have done.

Walking her deeper into the spare room, their feet soft against the hardwood floor, he didn't stop until the backs of her legs bumped against the bed. There he stepped back and drank in the sight of her, standing there so impossibly beautiful and courageous. He felt his eyes grow heavy, his body harden. "Earlier you asked me to let go."

The play of moonlight revealed a quick flare to her eyes, a streak of vulnerability so at odds with the Evangeline Rousseau he'd come to know, to crave, that he winced.

"Not now," she whispered, and he stepped closer, curling his hands around the soft, smooth curve of her hips.

"I want to hold on," he muttered as she tugged, and then they were on the bed, she on her back and he over her, not urgently like before, but with the gentle intimacy she deserved. With the time and tenderness they'd never had, never taken. He kissed her slow and deep, as he should have done the first time, making love to her with his mouth as his hands slid down to her breasts. With a soft moan she arched into him, her body practically vibrating as he slid his mouth down her neck and found her breasts.

"So beautiful," he murmured, first with little teasing kisses, like those she'd given him, then with a lingering drag of his tongue over her nipple.

This time he took it slow. This time he gave, rather than took. This time he savored, rather than let go. And when he slid his hand between her legs and found her hot and wet and ready, when he took her other hand in his and pushed inside of her, when he felt her close around him and saw her eyes turn languid, everything else fell away, leaving only her. *Evangeline.*

He slept.

Earlier there'd been moonlight. Now darkness spilled in through the window. Maybe an hour had passed. Maybe two or three. There was no clock in the bedroom—not really much of anything, Evangeline realized, glancing around. The bed was big and sturdy, a queen, with a simple striped comforter. The sheets, still stiff, were obviously new. There was a small table beside the bed, a lamp, an armoire across the room.

She was quite sure if she opened the doors, she would find nothing inside.

It was that way almost everywhere in Gabe's house—the one he'd shared with Val—as if every room had been scrubbed clean with the rigor of a crime scene....

And maybe it had. But not by the police, she knew. There'd been an investigation, yes. And Val's files had been confiscated. But the police would not have cleaned. The police would not have scrubbed. That had been Gabe.

The image rocked her, of Gabe alone in this house that had the potential to charm. She could see him, a big man in a small cage, the curtains closed, music pounding, scrubbing as a woman might in the shower after a sexual assault.

But Val's treachery had run deeper.

At the time, Evangeline had told herself Gabe had gotten nothing more than he deserved. She'd stayed on the sidelines and watched, listened, trying to convince herself it was better this way. That it was easier to break an already broken man than one standing tall.

But, God, she'd wanted the whole Gabe back, the man who turned heads wherever he went, whose intensity vibrated through her even when she couldn't see him….

She shifted against him, savoring the strength of his body, the feel of the hair on his legs against her calves, his chest beneath her face. His shoulders rose and fell with his breath. His heart strummed at a steady rhythm. Her heart—

Through the darkness she lifted a hand to his face and let her fingertips feather against the whiskers at his jaw. Gabe letting go had damn near destroyed her. But Gabe holding on…

Her throat tightened. He'd loved her with a raw intensity that had seared clear to the bone, a devastating gentleness that had fed that walled-off place deep inside. She'd come to him to bring him down. She'd come to him to make him pay, make him hurt.

He had hurt and he had paid…for crimes that had nothing to do with him. And if Marcel Lambert had his way…

The thought punished. If Marcel Lambert had his way, Gabe would go right on hurting, because he would never know the satisfaction of avenging his father's death. But if Marcel Lambert didn't have his way, if Gabe kept pushing, if he kept baiting the trap, then Gabe would pay another price. A steeper one.

And so would Jimmy.

The veil of contentment crumbled, and suddenly she couldn't continue to lie there in the darkness, in his arms, not when her heart slammed violently against her ribs. He would wake up. He would know.

And then he would start to strategize.

Easing from his arms, Evangeline slipped from bed and looked around, but saw nothing with which to cover herself. Unless she wanted to slip back into her dress. Which she didn't. Instead, she padded quietly from the room and made her way into the narrow hallway. A larger room opened across from her. The master, she realized, but did not go inside.

The second door she came across belonged to a bathroom, and from it she grabbed a white towel, much like the one that had been draped around Gabe's shoulders upon her arrival.

But it was the third door that stopped her. It was closed.

She should have left it that way, she knew that. She should have kept right on moving, toward the kitchen, for a glass of water or milk. Or to the dining room, where she could study the black-and-white picture of Gabe's father and Marcel Lambert as young men—and the reproduction of the fabled stained glass.

She should not have put her hand to the knob. And she should not have turned, pushed inside. But something dark and dangerous drove her. For over ten years she'd been looking for any scrap of evidence to prove Gabe had tampered with the jury that had sent Jimmy away.

Stepping inside the small, paneled room, she took it all in, the old rolltop desk sitting on one side, the bookcases covering one wall, the two large wooden file cabinets on the other.

After Gabe had shut her out, she'd had to resort to more covert tactics. She'd gained access to his office downtown and had taken a few files. She'd done other things, tried to smoke him out of complacency. She'd followed him and sent carefully worded notes…she'd tried to break into his house….

Desperation, she realized. It could twist and contort. It could stain. She'd come to New Orleans to prove Gabriel Fontenot was not a man of the law.

In the process, she, herself, had abandoned the law she claimed to love.

Now she ran her hand along one of the bookshelves. It was here, everything she'd come to find….

Gabe came awake hard, jerking up in bed before he even realized where he was. His breath ripped through him and his heart pounded. The stillness was…wrong.

He knew before he looked, knew she was gone. She was too warm and the bed was too cold.

Earlier there'd been moonlight, but now there was only darkness. "Evangeline!"

With a violence he didn't understand, he swung to his feet and stood, flicked on the bedside lamp and started for the hallway.

The slinky black puddle beside the bed stopped him. Her dress, he realized, exactly where he'd left it.

"Evie?" he called, but then she was there, stepping from the shadows with her hair loose around her face and a thick white towel wrapped around her body, a glass in her hands.

"Hi, there," she said, and damn near eviscerated him with a smile. "Miss me?"

The sight of her standing there more naked than not, in his house, his towel, fired through him. "I thought you were gone."

"Not a chance," she said, closing the distance between them and pushing up on her toes. "Just thirsty."

He glanced down first at the water, then the towel. Then he lifted his hands and tugged. "Care to share?"

The towel dropped to the floor. "Not a chance," she said again, this time stepping into him and backing him toward the bed. "I'm a one-on-one kind of girl," she said with a playful push.

He let himself drop to the mattress, went back on his elbows as he watched her lean over him and tilt the glass.

The cool drizzle of water over his chest shocked—even as it seduced.

"Uh-oh," she whispered, and her eyes took on a slow gleam, "looks like I spilled."

He glanced at the water trickling down his chest, then up at her. "So you did."

"Maybe I'd better take care of that," she said with exaggerated solemnity. Never looking away, she set the glass on the table and reached for the lamp.

"No." The word practically tore out of him. "Leave it on," he said, stopping her with a hand to her forearm. If she turned out the light, there would be only darkness—and he'd had enough of that. Now he wanted to see.

"No," she said, moistening her lips.

He looked at the mischief curving her mouth and damn near came unglued. "No?"

"No," she repeated, twisting her wrist from his grip. "I don't want to wait, anymore."

Normally, he loved the game, the dance. But impatience pulled through him. "Wait for what?"

Her smile widened as she slid her hand toward the lamp. "To find out if the rumors are true."

"What rumors?" he asked with a dark suspicion, but she was still smiling, her eyes still gleaming.

"About your work ethic," she answered with a matter-of-factness that defied the fact they were inches apart and naked, that they'd spent the better part of the past three hours doing anything but work. "How good you are in the dark."

"Ah," he said, anyway, because he knew the rumor—and the truth. "Those rumors," he drawled, pushing up to join his hand to hers, as together they turned out the light and found darkness. "I'll let you be the judge."

Chapter 13

Evangeline liked being the judge. Thorough adjudicator that she was, she considered every nuance, every angle, every exception. She reviewed the evidence, asked for more.

It was almost sunrise before she rendered her verdict: *Guilty as charged.*

Gabe watched her at the old pine table with her hair pulled into a ponytail, eating a bowl of sugary cereal. She was close to thirty, but the way his long-sleeved LSU jersey dwarfed her made her look young and fragile in ways he'd never expected. Every time she glanced up at him with a spoon in her hand and a light in her eyes, his chest tightened.

Her eyes, he knew. It was there in her eyes....

"So the Robichauds fled France during the Reign of Terror," she asked, looking up from genealogy notes of his father's. "And your dad's family fled Nova Scotia during the Exile?"

A history buff, his father had been obsessed with distilling legend from legacy, fact from fiction. That's how he'd met Gabe's mother, through his obsession with finding the truth about the mystical depiction of the rapture. "Only two children escaped France," he said. "A boy and a girl."

"What happened to the rest of the family?"

He glanced at the detailed drawing of angels and demons, sin and salvation. "No one knows for sure, but it looks like they were executed within days of smuggling the children out of the country." Their holdings in Brittany had been ransacked, the private chapel torched, all trace of the family…extinguished. "When I was a kid my dad took us there. He thought actually being there he might be able to find out—"

"Did he?" she asked, scooping up another bite of cereal.

"No." Not about the fate of the Robichauds—or the stained glass. Many claimed there'd never been a mystical stained glass, that all the rumors about healing properties were just stories. But others, mainly the elders, they'd shown Gabe's dad pictures….

Again he looked at the drawing, the date on the bottom right corner: 1756.

"So allegedly the children smuggled out this piece of stained glass with them?" she asked.

"Allegedly." But others said the stained glass had been destroyed when the chapel was burned, just like so many other historical and religious treasures.

"And then it showed up here?" she said, reaching for her orange juice. "Sometime before the Civil War?"

Again, he answered vaguely. "Allegedly."

She took a long sip of juice, then set the glass back down. "I heard the stories," she said. "When I was a little girl. My grandmother used to tell me about the pirates and the voodoo queens, the beautiful young woman who could make sick people well."

He looked up from his dad's notes and found the morning light spilling across her face. Her smile was soft, the abrasion beside her mouth no longer quite as pronounced.

"But it wasn't just a story, was it?" she asked.

The tightening came so damn fast he almost winced. Because she'd come into his life only a few months before, it was easy to forget they shared a history. They'd both grown up on the myths and legends, the lore. "No," he said. "It wasn't."

"And your dad was one of the men searching for it," she said.

Obsessing was a better word.

"And the Lamberts—" she frowned "—where did they come in?"

"Funding." It was as simple as that. His father had been a driven man, but proud. He'd refused to accept funds from his wife's family. He'd already felt as though he wasn't quite good enough for the Robichaud princess. He'd wanted to prove his worth, to restore the family legacy—

"Gabe."

Her voice was soft and it ripped right through him.

"You don't have to do this."

And just like that the illusion of a man and woman sharing a leisurely breakfast after a night of lovemaking crumbled. He pushed back from the table and strode into the kitchen, poured a second cup of coffee. The trap had already been laid. The bait was in place. Soon, he would be able to prove it was Lambert who had turned on his father.

And she wasn't going to stop him.

"I know what I'm doing," he said as his phone rang. He grabbed it, saw the number blocked, answered it anyway. "Fontenot."

"Gabriel," the mechanical voice greeted. "How nice of you to answer."

Something was wrong.

Evangeline told herself she was only imagining things, letting her mind run in a dangerous direction, but as she stood under the warm spray of the shower, the cold refused to let go.

The phone had rung. He'd talked for a few minutes. He'd kept his back to her, his voice low. She hadn't been able to make out many words, just his clipped tone. "You're lying," she'd heard. And, "Like hell."

Then Gabe had hung up and turned to her and told her there was something he needed to do. He'd suggested she shower. He'd walked her to his bedroom, kissed her before closing the door. Kissed her hard and deep, with an intensity that should have brought back every mind-numbing memory of the way he'd made love to her the night before and the delicious realization that the rumor about Gabe and the dark was most definitely true.

But there'd been something different about the kiss, a hunger, a…desperation that stayed with her and haunted. She ran his bar of soap over her body and lathered his shampoo into her hair, stepped from his shower and reached for his towel.

Through the foggy bathroom mirror she saw her face and lifted her hand to the bruise beside her mouth. That was passion. That was intensity. And Gabriel Fontenot was not the kind of man to let go like that, to hold on like that, with someone he didn't trust.

But the phone call…

Telling herself she was being ridiculous, she towel-dried her hair and wrapped the thick white towel around her middle, opened the door.

The blast of cool air hit her so hard she almost doubled over. Shivering, she looked for the robe she'd left on the bed—but saw Gabe. He lounged in the doorway, fully dressed, a long-sleeved black button-down tucked into his jeans, socks and shoes on his feet…while she stood wet and practically naked.

"Look at you," he drawled, and then he was crossing toward her, his long stride destroying the distance between them. "A man could go his whole life and never even imagine…"

She'd spent the night making love with him. She'd come to him, refused to back down until he let go. And when he had, he'd come to her with an intensity that should have frightened and, instead, she'd thrilled, wanted more. She'd stepped into him, held on tight.

Now he closed in on her and, for a disjointed second, she almost stepped back. "Gabe—"

"Got a second?"

Maybe it was the glitter in his eyes. Or maybe it was the way he kept looking at her, as if he'd never seen her before. But her heart kicked hard. "Sure," she said, "just let me get dressed."

His smile was slow, languorous. "Why?" he asked,

and though he'd yet to touch her physically, her body ached. "Something you don't want me to see?"

The dare streaked through her, scratching at the lies that stood between them. She found a smile, anyway, and put her hand in his. "Show the way," she said.

He did. The warmth of his hand soaked into her palm as he led her across the hall, toward the room that had stood shut the night before. Her heart kicked hard as he opened the door and let her in, stood back while she moved inside. Morning light brought little change to the richly masculine room, except for the electronics. Last night his laptop had sat on his desk, turned off. Now a cursor blinked against a gray screen. And last night she'd barely noticed the television and stereo equipment.

Now, dark lines streaked across the screen, as though something had been paused.

"Wow," she said, turning and trying to smile. The rest of the house had been gutted. He'd stripped it bare, gotten rid of all traces of Val. But this room, with its rich woodwork and scattering of family photographs on the credenza, with the reading glasses sitting near the laptop, looked warm and untouched. "I've heard that every man needs his space but this is…gorgeous."

The glimmer in his eyes darkened. "We all have our little secrets," he said quietly. A few steps and he reached a small round table beside the leather sofa. There he picked up a remote control. "I spend a lot of time here," he said. "It's where I come to work…to think."

And she could see him, too, see Gabe seated at the old rolltop desk late into the night, his hair rumpled from his hands, working on a brief or outlining a closing argument.

"Go ahead, have a seat," he said, aiming the remote at the TV. "There's something I need you to see."

The words were innocuous. They should have warmed. She and Gabe had come a long way in twelve hours. He'd shared more than just his bed. He'd fixed her a bowl of cereal and poured her a glass of juice. He'd let her see his father's journals, had talked about his past. That he would invite her into his private world, that he would share with her…

But her throat went tight, anyway.

And then came the image on the screen. It was dark and grainy, but she could make out the outline of his desk, and the bookcases, the file cabinets.

And then everything just stopped.

Because she knew. Even before the silhouette crossed the screen, she knew what was coming. Every last shred.

Much as it had the night before, the room smelled of leather and furniture polish, of man; and much like the night before, cool air swirled against her bare skin. Then, it had been quiet, the large TV blank. Now a damning video played against the screen, her silhouette wrapped in a towel and moving through Gabe's office, looking and touching, sliding open drawers….

And Gabe, standing so horribly, brutally rigid.

He knew.

The reality of that sliced through her, hard and deep and fast, without mercy or reprieve. Just a few hours before he'd moved languidly over her and inside of her. Now he stood only a few feet away, not looking at her, every line of his body hard and unforgiving. The mouth that had skimmed her body, tasting and giving, condemned. And his eyes…

They were trained on the television, but even without him looking at her, the derision there had the power to freeze.

She'd always known this moment would come. But she'd thought it would be on her own terms, at a time and place of her choosing. But never like this. Never here, now, with her body flushed from the last time they'd made love and, courtesy of a security camera, she'd never even suspected.

"Pretty fascinating, huh?" His tone was casual, but she recognized it in a heartbeat, that deceptively, lethal banter that always, always preceded the kill.

Classic Gabe, he'd kept his cards to his chest, until it was time to annihilate.

The movement of her hands was automatic, lifting to the ends of the towel and pulling it tighter. "Gabe…" It took effort, but she didn't let her voice shake. "This isn't what you think."

The irony staggered. Of all the lies she *had* told, of all the wrongs she had perpetrated, that he would learn the truth through something so purely innocent. Once she would have given almost anything to have access to his office, his files.

Last night she had. But instead of looking for evidence to condemn, she'd looked for any shred of information that might shed light on who really had gotten to the jury all those years before.

He lifted the remote and paused the tape, leaving the image of her opening one of his desk drawers frozen between them.

Then he turned to her, and she saw. For months she'd wanted him back, the Gabe from before, the one who'd vanished when his world blew up around him. He stood there now, but she saw only a stranger, a man no longer broken, but glued back together so tightly there were no cracks.

"Tell me," he said, still using that same laissez-faire voice, that could so easily fry a witness before he even knew the fuse had been lit. "How much is Lambert paying you?"

Nothing prepared her. Not the voice she knew not to trust, not the slow gleam in his eyes. The question collapsed around her, sent her hand groping for the back of the sofa. "What?"

"Was this his plan all along?" he asked silkily, standing there fully dressed while she wore only a towel. "You as the backup, the cleanup hitter to sweep in when Val—"

"No!" The word tore out of her. "That's not—"

"I'll pay you more."

Her fingers dug deeper into the leather. "Pay me more?"

"Whatever he's paying you," Gabe said, "I'll double it. Tell him you've got me just where you wanted me, but tell me his endgame, what kind of trap he's laying—"

Shock made her knees want to buckle. But she didn't let herself move, except to breathe. Of all the scenarios she'd envisioned, after the way she'd given herself to Gabe last night, she'd never imagined he could actually think she was in cahoots with Marcel Lambert.

But she should have, she realized. Because that's how Gabriel Fontenot's mind worked. Nothing was isolated. There was always a master plan. Everything fit together.

"You're wrong," she whispered, knowing the time had come—but also knowing it was too late. "I'm not working for Marcel Lambert."

She'd played poker with him once before, had seen the way he would sit there so benignly, holding his cards, looking almost bored while everyone around him scrambled.

"Then, who?" he asked with all the interest of a

man watching his competitor's posture, while he held a royal flush.

"I'm not working for anyone," she said. "Anyone but myself."

The sunlight spilling in through the shutters exposed every hard line of Gabe's face, his body. But no flicker to his eyes and no twist to his mouth. He didn't lift a hand to his nose, didn't swallow, didn't give her any kind of reaction. Didn't give her anything.

"Rousseau is my mother's name," she said, as she'd rehearsed so many times before. "Her maiden name."

The darkening of his gaze was so slight she couldn't be sure she'd even seen it.

"My father was a Montrose." Hesitating, she let the name hang there between them. *Montrose.* How many times had Gabe spoken that name? Written that name? Typed arguments and signed documents, reports. "That's what's on my birth certificate," she said.

But he gave her nothing that indicated any kind of bomb had just gone off.

"James was his name," she said, feeling it all start to unravel, twelve years of pain and anger, of injustice and determination, of drive and sacrifice.

"And my *brother's*," she added, and this time her voice betrayed her, tightening on the words, threatening to break.

Gabe's eyes narrowed. "James…"

"Jimmy." It hurt to say his name. It hurt to remember. And for some ridiculous reason, it hurt to realize Gabe had no idea who she was talking about, that even if he wasn't the one who'd tampered with the jury, he could shred and move on, never look back. Never remember, never wonder. Never care. "Jimmy Montrose."

Maybe the stillness around him deepened. Or maybe that was the shadows. She didn't know, only knew that he didn't say anything, didn't give her anything, just kept watching her like the prosecutor he was.

"Damn it," she snapped. And she couldn't stand it one second longer, the way he stood there so removed and unaffected. She let go of the sofa and closed the distance between them.

"Doesn't that mean anything to you?" she asked, lifting her hands to his chest.

Finally he moved. He caught her wrists and held them, stared down at her not with the icy recrimination from before, but the slow heat of recognition.

Chapter 14

Her eyes.

Gabe didn't trust himself to move, to think, barely trusted himself to breathe. He was a man who prided himself on the ability to clear away the clutter and focus on truth. Details were everything. The way someone stood, whether they made eye contact. If a woman twirled her hair or a man rubbed his jaw.

The truth was in the details.

And Evangeline's truth glowed in her eyes.

"You were there," he murmured with a sick punch to his gut. He saw it now. He didn't know how the hell he'd been so blind before.

"In the courtroom," he said, not letting go, not looking away. "Every day."

Her throat worked. Her mouth flattened into that defiant line he'd once taken as a dare. "Watching," she said, but her voice was so quiet he felt more than heard it. "Listening." She paused, angled her chin even more fiercely. "Dying."

The sister. It had been his first case. He'd been on fire, eager to blaze down the path that would, one day, allow him to make sure his father's murderer didn't go unpunished. He could still remember the gangly kid from a nearby bayou town, not much younger than Gabe had been at the time. Under different circumstances, they might have been friends.

"Your eyes," he said, and the words were raw. Every day she'd been there, a young girl no more than eighteen or nineteen, sitting in the courtroom with her hair in a ponytail, watching.

Jimmy Montrose had gone to prison, but his sister had followed Gabe, slipping into his sleep and watching him there. Always, always watching.

She stood here now in his study, still watching, still condemning. "He was innocent," she said, but he no longer recognized her voice. It wasn't the attorney's voice, or the woman's voice. But the sister's voice. "He was innocent, but he went to prison, anyway."

And she'd come here, to New Orleans. *To him.*

"He wanted to be a doctor," she whispered with an aching tenderness that brought everything into sharper focus. "Just like our father. He had a life, *Gabe*. A fiancée and a future."

He looked down at his hold on her wrists, let his hands fall away. "Jesus."

Evangeline glared up at him, her body rigid and composed, as if she wore one of her designer suits, rather than almost nothing at all. "And I'd thought you took it from him…took everything."

He backed away from her, from the truth that kept right on slicing. "That's why you're here," he realized coldly. Here in New Orleans as an assistant district attorney. Here in his house, his towel, as his lover.

She shoved the tangled hair from her face.

"He was innocent, Gabe. Don't you get that? Don't you care? Jimmy was innocent! He didn't kill that woman."

"The evidence—"

"Was tampered with," she said, cutting him off. "Just like the jury. Didn't you ever think it was too easy? Too tidy?" she asked. "Well, I did. And so did others. A juror even contacted me, said she needed to tell me something, that something was wrong."

Ugly pieces fell closer. That case. He'd been so sure he would lose that case.

"She said there'd been a payoff…that she had proof." Eyes glittering, Evangeline stepped closer. "But she died, Gabe. She was killed the day she was supposed to meet with me."

"*Jesus.*"

"There were other things." Evangeline rolled on, revealing comments several of her professors had made and theories of a journalist, another juror ready to talk. Gabe heard it all, felt each allegation slash a little deeper, like a thin leather strip biting into flesh, baring a truth that sickened.

"So you crawled into my bed—" He bit the words out. *Just like Val.*

And once again, he'd been as blind as a goddamned newborn.

"No!" Her voice wavered on the word. She stepped toward him looking at him not with the defiance of before, but a pleading that stung like alcohol to a fresh wound. "It wasn't like that. Everything I told you last night was true. I came to New Orleans to make you pay. And I tried…but the more time I spent with you, the more I got to know you, the man you are, the more everything blurred and—"

He stiffened, didn't trust himself to…do anything. "You never said a word." That one reality just kept right on twisting.

"I couldn't! Not until I knew for sure. I'd spent so long believing you to be a monster, and then I couldn't stop thinking about you…wanting you. I…was afraid," she said, and again she moved, taking another step. "And all I could think was that I couldn't let Jimmy down like that."

He looked at her standing there and felt something inside him break.

"But when I walked by your office last night, when I opened the door and walked inside… I realized it wasn't to find something to use against you. Someone framed you, Gabe. I thought if I could find—"

The lame excuse fell on deaf ears. He turned from her and strode from the office, went into the spare room and grabbed her dress and panties. When he turned, he practically ran into her.

She stopped and lifted her hands, reached for his arms. "Gabe, I know you don't—"

He stepped back and held out her clothes, let go when she had no choice but to take them. "Trust me, *catin,* you don't want to touch me right now."

Here there were shadows. Here the blinds were still down, leaving virtually no light to leak through and spill onto the bed. Here everything personal had been scrubbed away. There was nothing of Val, nothing of—

Only the bed. Evangeline looked from the wad of clothes in her hands to the tangle of sheets on the bed. That was all that remained of the night before.

"Why not?" she asked, jerking her gaze away to glare up at him. All those cracks she'd thought glued tight...now she realized no amount of glue in the world could fix this. "You might hurt me?" she shot back, even though she was pretty sure that he didn't hear her. *Couldn't* hear her. "I don't think so, Gabe. That's not you."

The last thing she expected was for him to smile, slow and steely. "You sure about that?"

All that emotion she'd shoved inside, tried not to feel, blistered closer to the surface. "*Damn it,* Gabe! Stop it! I love my brother. I want his life back, his future. Is that so horrible?" Even as she flung the question, she knew what Gabe's answer would be. "Can't you see?" she asked as the truth, the small room, closed in on her. "Sometimes the world isn't as clear-cut as you want it to be. Sometimes people do the wrong things for the right reasons."

"Is that what you tell yourself? That if you're just a little bit guilty, it's okay?" His gaze dipped low over her body, as his hands had done only a few hours before. "Is that what you thought the first time you kissed me—" his gaze raked back to hers "—last night, when you went down—"

"I was wrong about you," she whispered. Holding the towel tightly, she backed away. Wrong to think some damage could be undone. That some wounds could heal. That it would matter to him that she no longer believed him guilty. "Wrong to come here, to think the invincible Gabriel Fontenot could ever see anything other than black-and-white."

A wince, a twitch of a muscle, the slight narrowing of his eyes—anything. That's all she wanted. Anything, no matter how small, to let her know that he heard. That he felt.

That he cared.

But he gave her only whitewashed, completely bleached-out words. "You want to know what I see?" His voice was dead quiet. "I'll tell you what I see. I see a woman who offered herself to me to further her own agenda, not just once, but twice."

Just as Val had done. The truth of that, the reality, shamed. The fact she'd been looking for evidence to prove his innocence, rather than his guilt, could not erase her bigger indiscretion.

Later, she told herself. Later she would fall apart. But not now. And never, ever in front of Gabe. Of everything she'd been wrong about, most of all, she'd been wrong about him. He wasn't the man she'd thought he was, the man she'd so foolishly believed him to be. Not the cutthroat attorney, and not the fiercely loyal, compassionate man.

He was broken, and he didn't want to be fixed.

"You see what you want to see," she said with another step back. "What you let yourself see." Her hands clenched the fabric of her dress so hard she wasn't sure blood still flowed. "Haven't you ever loved someone or something so much the consequences didn't matter?" Jimmy, she told herself. She was talking about Jimmy.

But deep inside, she knew the truth.

She was talking about Gabe.

"That wrong became right," she whispered, "and right became wrong?"

For a long hard moment he looked at her. Then he

moved. He walked toward her, kept right on walking as he passed her. Down the hall and into the living room, then out of sight. But she could hear him, hear his footsteps against the hardwood floor. And then she heard the creak of the front door opening.

Slowly, mechanically, she let the towel drop and pulled her dress over her head, yanked at the zipper, gave up when it stuck between her shoulder blades. She jerked on her panties, didn't care about her shoes.

And then she walked down the hall and through the living room, past the dining room where her cereal bowl and empty glass still sat on the table, past the kitchen and into the foyer, to where he stood with the screen door held open.

Then she walked past him and into the cool swirl of an early-morning breeze.

There was no reason to look back.

He watched her go. He watched her walk toward the old Mustang parked across the street—a car he'd seen before cruising down his street. Had seen parked outside. He'd always assumed it belonged to one of his neighbors.

Never once had he considered that it had belonged to Evangeline, that she'd sat there behind the darkly tinted windows, watching and waiting, planning her next move.

Sometimes people do the wrong things for the right reasons.

He watched her slip inside, heard the rumble of the engine override the warblers nesting in his pecan tree. With the screen door propped open and the cool air rushing against him, he watched the car drive away.

He should have gone inside then, but he couldn't stop staring at the dogwood tree he'd planted the year he moved into his house. The sapling had quadrupled in size since then. Now its branches draped under the weight of new blooms. All around his yard, all up and down the street, the blooms were everywhere, white sprigs and fresh bursts of green had replaced the gray. Next door, even Mrs. Miller's tulips and daffodils had lifted their faces to the sun.

It had all seemed to happen over freaking night.

He watched it all a few minutes longer, until the kids across the street raced out into the yard with a kite. He turned before Gracie and Rene could see him, closing the door quietly behind him. Then he went to the kitchen and walked to the stove. From the cabinet he retrieved a bottle of whiskey. In the dishwasher he found the crystal tumbler that had once belonged to his father. Standing there, in the Spartan kitchen that still smelled of goddamn vanilla and powder, he took off the lid and poured.

The scent hit him immediately. He lifted the glass and savored, rocked the glass and watched the amber liquid swirl.

Haven't you ever loved someone or something so much the consequences didn't matter?

The images flashed hard and fast, and then he wasn't in his kitchen anymore. Wasn't a man, but a boy. In his backyard with Jack and Saura—and Camille. They'd been making bets as to who would catch the most crawdads.

Then he saw his dad, walking up from the bayou behind their house with his hip-waders on, warning them that the water was deeper than usual. To be careful.

They'd gone, anyway…and Gabe had damn near drowned dragging Jack out of the water after he'd lost his balance on a rock and fell, hitting his head before slipping into the bayou.

That night there'd been gunshots.

And his father had died.

Slowly, Gabe lifted the tumbler to his lips. He'd loved. And he had forgotten about consequences. Funny thing was, they never forgot about him.

His hands were steady as he glanced down at the glass, then threw it across the kitchen. It hit the granite countertop and shattered.

"Grisly Murder Rocks New Orleans."

"Fontenot Wins First Case."

"Montrose Sentenced to Twenty Years."

Evangeline stared at the collection of newspaper articles. There were others, too, ten years' worth of articles about a rising star in the New Orleans district attorney's office. And pictures. Lots of them. She saw Gabe as he'd been back then, young and green, full of Southern charm and reckless confidence.

Mechanically, she sorted through the clippings and articles, until she came to the last one she'd tucked away, only a few months before. She saw Gabe's picture there, too, saw the indelible marks a decade in the criminal justice system had left on him. The cocksure young man from that first picture was gone, replaced by a stoicism she'd always believed to be part of the game he played. His bluff.

Now she realized it was how he survived.

"Fontenot on Unpaid Leave." That was the title of the article that had appeared two days after Val had been killed. There'd been little coverage of her betrayal, virtually no mention of the way she'd infiltrated Gabe's life with the sole intent of siphoning critical information about cases the D.A. was prosecuting to the highest bidder—in most cases, organized crime. The articles glossed over all that, concentrating on the scandal of linking a leak in the D.A.'s office to one of its finest. The fact that Robichaud blood ran through Gabe's veins only made it all the more juicy.

Next to the article sat the notebook in which she'd documented her investigation. At the bottom of the last page on which she'd written was a name and today's date.

Slowly she gathered her notes and returned them to her fireproof box, grabbed her purse and walked out the door to her car. Almost three hours had passed since she'd walked away from Gabe, but the adrenaline kept right on rushing. She'd showered again and dried her hair, put on makeup and dressed in a pair of tan slacks with a white, peasant-style blouse. Now she headed toward her meeting with juror number eight.

Maybe Gabe didn't know how to forgive. Maybe she'd been an idiot to let herself fall for a man who couldn't see anything but black-and-white. And maybe he was right, that there was no such thing as only a little bit guilty. In bending the laws to suit her own purposes, she'd compromised more than herself. She'd compromised her brother—and the man she'd come to love. But someone had gone to great lengths to convince her Gabe had tampered with Jimmy's jury.

She owed it to all of them, to Gabe and Jimmy, to herself, to find out who—and why.

Half an hour later she turned off Canal Street and into the department store parking garage. Juror number eight was upstairs, in the china department. They would meet casually….

Opening her door, she stepped into the cool shadows and started to turn—saw him too late.

The blow came hard and fast. Staggering, she slumped into the front seat and blinked only once before the darkness came—bringing with it the freezing realization that juror number eight was not the one who'd arranged this meeting.

"*Les Bon Temps Roulez.*"

Gabe stared at the bold headline, then the accompanying picture. Of Evangeline—and Marcel Lambert. The man had his arm around her. They both smiled. The caption noted that the desire to rebuild New Orleans made strange bedfellows: even the woman the D.A. had handpicked to prosecute Darci Falgoust's murder had turned out with her checkbook to support Marcel and his campaign to bring back New Orleans.

The good times roll.

Over four hundred thousand dollars had been raised and the credit was being heaped on Lambert as liberally as his crawfish étoufée over rice. There was no mention of his arrest or the charges pending against him, the upcoming trial.

Gabe dragged his finger along the curve of Evangeline's dress, the same dress that had been pushed up over her hips when they'd made love the first time—and the same dress he'd slipped from her body sometime later.

The same dress he'd handed to her in a wad that morning.

He blocked the memory before it could form any further. He didn't want to go back. But the slow freezing burn kept right on incinerating everything in its path.

Sometimes people do the wrong things for the right reasons....

Very slowly, very deliberately, he pulled the sports section over the society page and glanced at his phone, saw that he had plenty of battery. The night was young. There was plenty of time for the call to come. She would—

Not she. *He.* He would call. Lambert would. The rumors would have reached him by now; that Gabe had picked up the pieces of his father's obsession. Lambert would call and take the bait, make arrangements to walk into Gabe's trap. And then Gabe would close the circle that had opened the night he'd lost his father.

The double beep from his computer came less than a minute later. He swung toward his laptop and moved it out of sleep mode, clicked open the e-mail box—and saw the new message.

"Gabriel, *frere*—" brother "—something you forgot to tell me?"

The voice came at him like a lazy slap, and he looked up to see Jack lounging in the doorway. He and John had shown up shortly after six. They'd unearthed a little more information, had learned that the girl who'd sent Gabe and Evie to the cottage had been none other than Darci's younger sister.

Gabe clicked on the message, waited for it to open. "Tell you about what?"

"Oh, I don't know," Jack drawled, his eyes gleaming. And then he lifted his hand. "Maybe about these?"

The stilettos came into view just as the e-mail opened. She'd been barefoot, he remembered. She'd walked across the street in her wrinkled black dress, barefoot.

Crushing the memory, he glanced at his laptop and saw the words:

You have something of mine—I have something of yours.

Everything inside of him went cold.

"If I didn't know better…" Jack was saying, but Gabe heard nothing after that.

Tomorrow morning we will trade.

For over two decades Gabe had been waiting. And for over two decades he'd been anticipating. Now the low hum inside him grew louder with each additional line he read. There were instructions, very detailed, very specific.

He was to arrive at an abandoned warehouse in the morning, with the stained glass. He was to tell no one. At the warehouse, he would hand the relic over. Then, and only then, he would receive something very important to him.

"…shrimp po'boys?"

He blinked, forced himself to look at the doorway, where John now stood beside Jack.

If you tell anyone, the deal is off.

These men were his friends, but at the moment, with their eyes narrowed and concentrated on him, they looked all cop.

Slowly, he stood.

If you don't show, the offer is over.

"Po'boys would be great," he said.

If you don't produce, you'll never know what happened to her.

He reached for his mouse and scrolled lower—saw the picture. Of her. Evangeline. Lying in a fetal position. Her eyes closed.

Her hands and feet bound.

"Gabriel—" Jack said, and Gabe blinked, saw his friend moving toward him.

The roaring came from all directions, but with discipline born of a single gunshot, he logged out of his e-mail and closed his laptop, stood and rounded his desk, joined his friends. They would go out for po'boys. They would eat; the other two would drink.

Gabe would plan. The trap had been his. But with seven simple words, Marcel Lambert had turned the tables.

You'll never know what happened to her.

Chapter 15

Condemned.

Gabe slid his 9mm into his waistband and stared at the sign tacked outside the old warehouse.

It had not been there the week before.

Frowning, he reached for the door and stepped inside. Seven days before there'd been only darkness. He'd moved through the shadows, slipping between crates and ignoring the stench of decay, drunk on the conviction that soon Marcel Lambert would fall.

In the process, he'd found Evangeline—and a truth that damn near eviscerated him. He could still see her as she'd been that night on the concrete beneath him, with her hair spilled around her face and her eyes glowing with courage and defiance and something else, a light, a confusion that he hadn't understood then. But did now. Too well.

Through the filter of early-morning light, he pressed deeper inside, cataloging what the shadows had tried to hide: a shopping cart of threadbare clothes, a pile of mismatched shoes, empty cans of beer and broken whiskey bottles. A stack of waterlogged photos and the shell of a grand piano. An empty bag of dog food.

In the world before Katrina, the sight would have puzzled him. But the people of New Orleans no longer questioned things out of place. The floodwaters had swirled everything in their path into one big gumbo. Even the dead had not stayed put.

The image formed before he could stop it, of the photo embedded in the e-mail. Of Evangeline. Lying so horribly still. He'd bluffed his way through dinner with Jack and John, had sat there stone-faced while everything inside of him had twisted and tangled.

Haven't you ever loved someone or something so much the consequences didn't matter?

"I'm here," he called, working his way among the crates. He knew he was being watched, just as he knew it was no coincidence that Lambert had chosen this warehouse. It was strategy, another piece of the invisible game they'd been playing since the day Gabe had joined the district attorney's office.

Over his shoulder he had a backpack. Inside, he had a tape recorder. "I'm ready," he invited.

Only silence greeted his words.

Sludge covered the floor, but he barely smelled the stench. With the same discipline that had allowed him to eat a po'boy and drink iced tea without giving Jack or John a clue that anything was wrong, he forced himself not to think of Evangeline the last time he'd seen her, the hurt in her eyes as she'd walked out the door.

Because if he did, if he allowed himself to see and re-member, to feel, he would drown in all the shades of gray he'd never allowed himself to see. The shades that made him realize her sins were no different than his. And now, more than ever, he needed the focus—without it, he would lose more than Marcel Lambert.

He'd lose the woman who'd made him realize that when you loved someone, consequences didn't matter.

Everywhere he turned, she was there. He could see her as she'd been that night the week before, when she'd twisted beneath him and he'd realized she was the one who'd driven him to the ground. When she'd stared up at him with those bottomless gray eyes, trying to pretend he hadn't hurt her.

Later that night, when he'd tucked her into bed.

And the next morning when she'd walked into her living room, with her hair tangled and the oversized T-shirt revealing her long, long legs.

And so many other times not just in the past week, but before, during the fall, when he'd found himself seeking her out. When he'd tried not to want her, but had—

"Hello, Gabriel."

The voice, quiet and deceptively urbane, came from behind him. He reached for his gun and turned, found Marcel Lambert standing between two stacks of crates. In his khaki slacks and black button-down, with his graying hair neatly combed and his cheeks ruddy, he looked ready to stroll onto the set of a morning news show and begin cooking. "Marcel."

"How nice of you to join me," Marcel said, then nod-ded toward the 9mm. "But I'm afraid I can't allow you to have that."

"Of course." Gabe tossed the weapon to the floor.

Once, he'd held the illusion that lawyers operated in the courtroom, that they meted out justice after the crimes had been committed. But once again he stood on the other side of the crime, the before. This time, he was prepared.

"Very good." Lambert used his foot to drag the gun toward him, stooped to pick it up. "Now there's really no reason to dawdle, is there? Why don't you just go ahead and give me what I want, then I'll give you what you want."

Evangeline. The urge to charge Lambert blindsided Gabe. He had on Kevlar. He could survive a blow to the chest.

But he did not allow himself to move. "Then what? You just go your way, and I go mine?"

"That all depends."

"On what?"

"How badly you want her to live."

This time the words weren't benign. Gabe surged forward, stopped when Lambert lifted the gun.

"Now, now," the older man said. "Let's not get ahead of ourselves."

Twenty years before, Gabe had only been a boy. He'd had no choice but to watch and to wait, to plan. But now he was a man and he was done playing Lambert's game.

"No deal." Grabbing the backpack slung over his shoulder, he opened it and turned it upside down, revealed there was nothing inside. "If you want what I have, you're going to have to let her go, first."

Lambert lifted an eyebrow. "And if I do? If I give you what you want, you'll give me what your father stole from me?"

Gabe's smile was slow. "Is that what you've told

yourself all these years? Is that how you justify murder, by pretending my father stole something from you?"

Lambert eyes gleamed. "You think I'm the one pretending?" The question was measured. "Tell me, then. Tell me where you found the stained glass—and tell me where it is now."

"Somewhere safe," Gabe said. "Somewhere you won't find it, until I'm ready." The microrecorder was running. Every word was being documented. He had only to draw the other man deeper into the past, get him to talk about—

The laughter stopped him. They stood in the shadows of the condemned warehouse, Marcel Lambert holding a gun on Gabe, Gabe holding Lambert's freedom in his hands, and Lambert laughed.

"Ah, dear, boy," he said, "your daddy could have learned a lot from you."

The tightening started low, spread fast.

"You do know how to bluff," Lambert went on, "but we both know you don't have the stained glass."

Now it was Gabe's turn to smile, slow and easy. "Really? I suppose that's why you're here? Why you wanted to meet? To trade?"

The other man shook his head. "Not at all."

"Then—"

"I wanted to see your face when you realized your father wasn't the saint you've made him out to be."

Everything inside of Gabe stopped.

"Imagine my surprise," Lambert continued, "when I start hearing rumors about the real reason Gabriel Fontenot has been low profile the past few weeks. That he took up his father's obsession—that he *found* his father's obsession." Gun steady, Lambert stepped closer.

"Imagine my surprise, since I was there the night the stained glass was destroyed."

Gabe didn't let himself move. Couldn't. Because all he could see was the yellow tape streaming through his father's study. His Uncle Edouard had been there, talking with his mother. He'd been asking about some broken glass found near his father's desk.

"You're lying." But a bad, bad feeling wouldn't stop twisting.

"We were supposed to be partners."

Gabe had figured that much out, despite the fact Marcel denied any affiliation with Troy Fontenot. Gabe had a picture that proved otherwise. There'd been four of them, his father and Jack's father, the two Lambert brothers.

Now only Marcel remained. He stood only a few feet away, with a gun in his hand and a glassy sheen to his eyes. "He took my money," he went on, "said he'd used it to fund his search. And I believed him even after the rumors started, the rumors that he'd found the stained glass months before, and that he and that no-account Savoie used my money to gamble and drink."

"My father didn't gamble," Gabe said.

But Jack's father had. Gator Savoie had always been convinced easy street was one hand of cards away.

"I'd caught them red-handed, found him and Gator holed up one night…with the stained glass."

Gabe took an instinctive step back.

"I'd demanded that they give it to me. It was mine. I'd paid for it."

Denial came hot and hard and fast.

"There was a struggle," Lambert said. "The stained glass…shattered."

Camille had been there. She'd talked about loud voices—and something breaking.

"Your father was beside himself. He pulled a gun," Lambert said. His voice was softer now, further away. "There was another struggle."

And the gun had gone off.

Lambert didn't say the words, but Gabe heard them, had lived them.

"So, yes, Gabriel." With the words, Lambert once again smiled. "I was there when your father died. But it was his own greed that killed him. If he'd stuck to our bargain—"

"We'll leave that to a court of law." The words practically tore out of Gabe. It wasn't the confession he wanted, but a jury would easily see through the lies.

"No," Lambert said, "I'm afraid we won't."

Gabe looked from Lambert to the gun, to the crates surrounding him. His timing would need to be perfect—

"You still don't see, do you?" Lambert asked. "I'm a smart man, Gabriel, a believer in insurance. You really think I don't know you have a plan?" He curved his finger around the trigger. "I've always known, Gabriel. Always known the first chance you got to avenge your father, you would come after me. And so I've taken measures to make sure that can never happen."

Evangeline. A quick lunge to the right, and the crates would fall—

"And I've got quite an arsenal, too, Gabriel, beginning with the first case you ever prosecuted."

Gabe looked back toward Lambert, but the shadows kept right on bleeding, until there was no line between light and dark.

"The evidence is in a secure location," Lambert

rolled on, "with instructions, should anything happen to me. It's all there—the large sums of money paid to three jury members. The testimony of two others about the young prosecutor who tried to coerce them first with money, then with threats—"

The warehouse started to spin. *He was innocent, Gabe. Don't you get that? Don't you care?*

"And locked away in your own files is the transcript of an interview you conducted with a friend of young Jimmy Montrose's, in which she plainly states Jimmy was with her."

Didn't you ever think it was too easy? Too tidy?

"Of course, you and I know you never conducted that interview, but what's a small detail like that?"

All those shadows shifted, those from the night his father was killed and the day Jimmy Montrose was convicted, the devastation in Evangeline's eyes, swirling around Gabe like the floodwaters that had decimated his city. There was only one reason Lambert would confess this fully, when he had to suspect Gabe was recording every word.

He had no intention of Gabe leaving the warehouse alive.

"It's time for your crusade to end," Lambert said, backing away. Eyes on Gabe, he removed a small electronic device from his pocket. "You can come after me, of course. And you might even catch me." With his forefinger, he depressed a small black button. "But know that if you do, she dies."

The words slammed into Gabe, stopped him cold. And from somewhere deep in the warehouse came a low hiss.

"And so I really must be going now," Lambert concluded, still mildly as he pulled something from a small case. "Because you see, there isn't much more time. Now, give me the recorder."

"You're lying." Gabe gritted out the words, but, already, he was coughing, his nostrils and throat burning.

Lambert lifted a mask to his face. "You are, of course, welcome to come after me," he said as the pieces fell together, the steady hiss and the mask, the tightening of his throat…

Gas.

"But in seven minutes, anything in this warehouse will be dead—including your Evangeline.

"And if you don't believe me," Lambert added, "you have only to see the proof for yourself." He used his foot to push a small box to Gabe—then continued backing away. "The recorder."

Gabe grabbed his shirt and brought it to his face, used it to breathe through the fabric. Then he dropped to his knees and opened the box, saw the small computer screen—and Evangeline. She lay beside a crate, curled on her side with her hands and feet bound.

"She's your only chance, isn't she?" Lambert mocked. "Your only chance at winning—and the only thing standing between you and the revenge you've wanted for almost a quarter of a century. Her testimony is the only way anyone will believe you over me… Of course, if you do get her out, I'll be long gone."

Gabe's eyes burned and his mouth started to swell. "Evie!" At his voice, she stirred, but the gag in her mouth prevented her from answering.

"It's not so clear-cut, anymore, is it?" Lambert taunted with another step back. "Come after me, and she dies—and who do you think the authorities will believe? You, the A.D.A. on leave, who destroyed evidence that would have cleared me? Or the man who helped raise half a million dollars for restoration?"

Gabe's vision blurred.

"You're the one who lured me here," Lambert reminded, his voice muffled by the gas mask. "The rumors are everywhere. You're the one who pretended to have what your father stole from me. And to what end? Just to taunt me?"

Gabe staggered to his feet. All his life there'd never been any wrong choices for the right reasons. But now...

Lambert was right there. He could go after him. He could avenge his father.

But in doing so, Evangeline would die.

"Do it, Gabe," Lambert invited as Gabe narrowed his eyes and tossed the other man the recorder containing his confession. "Follow me," he taunted, retrieving it. "Tell everyone what a monster I am. Have your revenge...but know that her death is on your hands."

"Evie!" She could be anywhere. Lambert was a smart man. It would have been logical to hide her as far away as possible—

Which meant Lambert might also have hidden her as close as possible.

"Give me something!" he roared, then he was running, or at least trying to run. "Evie!"

He darted around the old piano and saw Lambert backing toward the door with the gun held in front of him. "You son of a bitch!"

And from somewhere to his left came a loud crash.

Lambert swung toward the noise, and Gabe had his opening. He was a lawyer by training, but a Robichaud by birth. And he wasn't about to let Marcel Lambert win. He charged into the nearest stack of crates and sent them tumbling. Then he rammed into the next stack. And then the next.

The crates crashed down, starting a chain reaction. Through the free fall he saw Lambert twist away and start to run—then he heard the grunt as the other man crashed down.

"Evie!" She was the one who made the noise. She was the one who'd given him the opening. Staggering, he ran toward the fallen crates and found Lambert shoving at them. The 9mm lay several inches from his hand.

Grabbing it, Gabe lifted it to Lambert. "Toss me the gas mask."

The other man's eyes flared, panic for the first time bleeding in. *"Now."* He wasn't a man to shoot in cold blood, but Evangeline's life hung in the balance. "Where would you like me to start?" he asked. "Your thigh? Or your hand?"

Pinned beneath three crates, Marcel glared at Gabe as he lifted his hands and pulled off the mask, tossed it to Gabe. "It's already too late," he coughed. "You'll never find her."

"You better hope that's not true." Grabbing the mask, Gabe pivoted and ran. "Evie!" he shouted. "Give me a noise!"

Yanking the mask over his face, he sucked in clean air and tried not to stagger. But his eyes watered and his throat burned.

He heard it then, a thump. Twisting, he reached for his phone and stabbed out a number on his speed dial.

The second he kicked aside a crate blocking his path, he saw her. She still lay on her side, but her eyes were closed. And she wasn't moving.

Jerking at the mask, he dropped to his knees and

reached for her. "Jack!" he roared into the phone, but then the doors on all sides burst open simultaneously and the shouting started.

He scooped up Evangeline and ran toward the light cutting in through the nearest door. "Breathe," he rasped, pressing the mask to her face. *"Breathe!"*

"Gabriel!"

Looking up, he saw Jack and Cain and his Uncle Edouard running through the fading shadows.

"Get Lambert," he instructed as his knees tried to buckle. "B-back by…the p-piano."

Cain and his uncle ran past him. Jack stayed, reaching for Evangeline. But Gabe wouldn't give her up, couldn't let go. Not this time. Instead, Jack fell into step beside them, bracing Gabe as he helped them outside.

The squad cars and fire engines stunned Gabe. The paramedics were already rushing toward them.

And Evangeline started to cough.

Staggering, he felt Jack catch him. And even through eyes that wouldn't stop stinging, Gabe saw him grin. "You didn't really think we'd leave all the fun to you, did ya, *frère?*"

They knew. He'd been so sure that he'd bluffed his way through dinner, but his friends had known.

"Evie…" Going down on his knees, he worked at the rope that bound her ankles, her wrists. There were welts. "Come on, baby, come back to me…."

Her eyes, huge and dark and the most amazing shade of gray, slowly opened. "Gabe," she whispered. *"You're here."*

The rushing started then, deep inside like a strong punishing wind. He'd been so damn blind. He'd turned his back on her when he should have held on tight. He'd refused to hear what she said, to listen and understand.

He'd refused to see anything other than his own vision of the world and, in doing so, he'd almost lost her.

"I'm here," he said, taking her hand and drawing it to his mouth. She lay against the concrete, with her lips dry and her cheeks pale. The skin at her wrists and ankles red and swollen and angry.

But Gabe saw only beauty and a raw courage that had sent him to his knees. "And I'm not going anywhere."

The smell of coffee woke her. Once, the rich aroma would have made Evangeline smile and stretch, lazily wander toward the kitchen.

Now she came awake fast and hard. Her heart slammed as it all rushed back, every damning detail—standing almost naked in Gabe's study, watching the video of her sneaking into his office, the hard gleam in his eyes when he'd realized who she really was and why she'd infiltrated his life. That she'd had an agenda all along.

She'd tried to make him understand....

Come on, baby...

The meeting with juror number eight that turned out to be a trap. The blow to the back of her head and the darkness, the small room where she'd been kept. The warehouse. The sound of her name on Gabe's voice. He'd sounded worried—

Come back to me!

He'd emerged from the shadows at a dead run and scooped her into his arms, run into the sunshine. There he'd gone down on his knees and held her, refusing to let go even when the paramedics rushed over.

I'm not going anywhere!

Time fragmented. There'd been shouting and running, a swarm of police and firefighters. Marcel Lambert on a stretcher. An ambulance. Gabe holding her hand, never letting go.

Now darkness filled the room. Her room, she remembered. Gabe had brought her back to her loft. Blinking against the dryness of her eyes, she glanced at the bedside clock and saw the green glow of the numbers: 11:13 p.m.

Only a week before she'd awakened much the same way. Then she'd scrambled out of bed and onto her knees, made sure her box had not been disturbed. But now she remembered reaching for it sometime earlier that day and handing it to Gabe.

Slowly she slipped out of bed. And slowly she reached for the glass of water and took a long sip. But she didn't reach for the pain pills. She didn't need them—and knew he didn't, either.

With Simon weaving between her legs, she made her way into the hallway, drawn by the sound of a late-night talk show. And, much like the week before, she found him standing in front of her old curio cabinet, with a mug in one hand and a baseball in the other. A wrinkled gray button-down hung untucked against his jeans.

"You're still here," she whispered, and from deep inside came a quickening that should have frightened. But didn't.

He twisted toward her, all rumpled six foot two of him, but this time he didn't frown. He smiled. It was one of those slow, easy, classic Gabe smiles, the kind that could touch without even a flicker of physical contact. "I told you I wasn't leaving you."

The hoarse words did cruel things to her heart. It

strummed low and hard and deep, carrying with it a hope she never would have imagined possible only twenty-four hours ago.

"That's what you said last week," she pointed out as cool air rushed against her bare legs.

Gabe's eyes met hers. "What is it they say about history repeating itself?"

It was impossible to look at him and not remember his touch, the feel of his hands and his mouth, of his body moving against hers. The way it had felt to lie in his arms after making love, to hear his heart and his breath, to feel the warmth of his body.

The way he'd stood there with the screen door held open, his eyes fixed on the pecan tree as she'd walked barefoot from his house.

"I'm ready for it to stop," she said. There'd been enough repeating, enough mistakes. And for all that she'd planned her infiltration into Gabe's life, she had no contingency plan for this. No idea what to say to the man who knew her secrets, but who'd risked his life for hers, anyway, who'd been willing to forfeit the goal that had stripped him of his childhood and shaped him into the man he'd become, who'd stayed with her and held her, who'd insisted on watching over her.

Who watched her now.

Only the day before, the dark blue of his eyes had glittered. In them she'd seen the impact of her lies and from them she'd felt a slow bleed of cold.

His eyes didn't glitter now. And in those cobalt depths she saw no lies, but a truth that made her throat tighten—and a warmth she'd never expected. Glancing from her to the baseball, he returned it to the curio cabinet—then stunned her by destroying the distance between them. His hand came next, slow and steady up to her face. His touch, excruciatingly gentle. "Dizzy?"

She swallowed. "No."

His fingers feathered against a tender spot at her temple. "This hurt?"

Not there. "I'm fine really," she said, trying to pull away, to put the distance back between them. Because what hurt was his touch. What hurt was the memory.

But then he spoke again, three little words, and everything just stopped, "So is Jimmy."

Almost a week had passed since her concussion, but the room tilted, anyway. "Jimmy?"

Gabe eased the hair from her face, tucking it behind her ears. "I've been on the phone with the warden," he said, and though it was the attorney's voice, full of conviction and authority, it was also the man's voice, the tender voice, the one with warmth…the one that came with absolution and acquittal. "And a federal judge. And the governor."

It took a heartbeat for it all to register. "My God—"

"He was roughed up pretty bad, but he's going to be fine."

Evangeline closed her eyes, said a silent prayer of thanks.

"He's going to be free, too," Gabe said, and then her eyes were wide-open and staring into his.

Vaguely it came back to her, what Gabe had told her as he'd held her hand en route to the hospital. Marcel Lambert was the one who'd arranged her brother's conviction. He was the one who'd tampered with the jury—who'd tampered with her and with Gabe.

All this time, he'd been quietly manipulating them all. "He killed your father," she whispered, and with the words her heart hurt. Gabe had known. All along he'd known, but there hadn't been a damn thing he could do. "And stole Jimmy's future. And Darci...he put us on a collision course—"

The blue of Gabe's eyes darkened. "I don't want to talk about Lambert," he said, taking her hands.

Warmth. It bled into her and through her. "Gabe—"

But he shook his head before she could finish, threaded his fingers through hers. "All my life it's been black-and-white, a choice is right or wrong, a person is guilty or innocent."

He stood there so tall and strong, but in his words she heard the boy he'd been.

"And then you came along," he said, and this time she saw it in his eyes, too, the boy who'd built forts and caught crawdads, who'd terrorized his sister.

Until the night his father was executed.

"And held up a mirror, made me see what I'd never let myself see; that I'm a hypocrite."

The words went through her like a knife to the gut. "No—" That word was strong, sure "—you're not a hypocrite."

But she wasn't even sure he heard her. "You were right," he said, "about everything. Nothing is that simple—not my father's murder or your brother's conviction, your need for justice—"

"Or yours," she whispered.

"Or mine." On a hard sound from low in his throat he released her hands and brought his to her face, touched with a sense of discovery so raw, it hurt to breathe. "I was wrong to shut you out," he stunned her by saying. "I was wrong to turn my back on you, to not think what it must have been like for you, knowing your brother was rotting in prison for a crime he didn't commit and thinking, believing—"

"Gabe." She could see what this was doing to him. "You don't have to do this."

But he kept going. "After Val—" his voice thickened and she knew what it cost him to talk about Val "—I didn't trust myself. My God," he ground out. "Even after I found out about the Internal Affairs investigation, even after I knew everything was just a lie—"

"No—" with a hard slam of her heart she reached for him "—no—that's just it, *we* were never a lie...."

"I still wanted you." He rolled right on. Then, so quiet she barely heard him, "I still wanted you."

Regret stabbed in from all directions, bringing with it a darker truth. "And then history repeated itself."

But Gabe shook his head. "No," he said. "Only in a black-and-white world. You came after me for the same reason I went after Lambert. Because you thought I hurt someone you loved."

She stilled.

"You were right," he said, and the rushing started again, deep inside. "Last week, when you said I would have gone after someone just like you did... Christ, I did, Evie. I did the exact same thing. For twenty years I've been on a crusade that has nothing to do with due process. I've broken rules and laws—and I would've done more."

Slowly, she lifted her hands to his face. "Gabe, that man killed your father."

"And if I'd killed him? He'd still be dead and I'd still be a murderer. In a court of law—"

"You didn't kill him."

His eyes glittered. "I can hardly remember a day

when I didn't want to see Lambert fall. But there in that warehouse, when I realized that in trying to lure him into a trap, he'd lured me into one, that he had you there, that he wanted me to choose between him and you—" Something hard and dark and sharp flashed through his eyes. He squeezed them shut, opened them a long second later. "There was no choice."

Her heart kicked hard. "Gabe."

"There was no choice!" he said again, and this time the words were rough and raw. "You, Evie. You're all that matters."

The words humbled her. She looked away, looked at the coffee table where the lockbox she'd given him sat, open now, its contents in neat little stacks. "I should have told you the truth as soon as I'd realized how wrong I was."

With his hands, he eased her face back to his. And with his words, he shattered. "Before you walked out the door," he said, sliding his thumb along her lower lip, "you asked me if I'd ever loved anything so much that the consequences didn't matter."

She wasn't sure why she stepped back.

"The answer is yes." He moved toward her even as she took another step back. "I would have let him walk—I would have let him get away with everything, as long as I didn't lose you again."

Her breath caught. "You're not going to lose me."

"That's how much I love you," he said, and then he was there, reaching for her again, and this time she didn't back away…knew she would never back away from him. Not ever, ever again. *"You."*

Epilogue

Night bled through the window overlooking the back-yard. Soon heavy brocade curtains would frame the gaping darkness, but not tonight. There hadn't been enough time.

The paint was still wet.

Evangeline lowered the roller and surveyed her handiwork. The muted olive lent the room a warmth the white walls had not.

But she'd seen the potential. From the moment she and Gabe had stepped into the hundred-year-old Acadian-style house in the Garden district, they'd known they were home. There was work to be done, lots of it. But it was work they both embraced.

Gabriel Fontenot was a man of many talents; that was something she'd always known. But not even that knowledge had prepared her for the way he'd rolled up his sleeves and gotten to work, tearing out run-down cabinetry in the kitchen and installing new cabinets, even an island and breakfast bar. He'd added crown molding in the living and dining room. He'd torn up the old carpet and put down hardwood floors.

But the bedroom was her domain.

At least for now.

Spying a few speckles of white, Evangeline picked up a smaller roller and dipped it in paint, stepped toward the wall and finished what she'd started five hours before, when she'd shooed Gabe out of the house. D'Ambrosia and Cain had conspired with her. Savannah had stopped by with a bottle of wine earlier, but Saura had not been with her. She was out of town again, still working some big secret case that she wasn't yet allowed to talk about.

Above the classic rock jangling from the iPod Gabe had surprised her with, Evangeline never heard the double beep of the security system. But her heart kicked the second the bedroom door pushed open and she spun.

He stood there without moving, looking at her as if she wore some kind of skimpy little negligee, rather than an oversized paint-splattered New Orleans Saints T-shirt. The cobalt of his eyes gleamed and his mouth, shadowed by a few days' worth of whiskers, curved into a smile.

And for a moment, it was all Evangeline could to do breathe.

After so many months of doubt and deceit, of lies and betrayals and secret agendas, sometimes it was still hard to believe that they'd found the other side—and each other. Five weeks had passed since the morning Gabe had found her in the warehouse—and the night they'd both given each other the gift of their love. Since then…a lot had happened. Marcel Lambert was awaiting trial. And Jimmy was free. It had all happened so fast, a matter of days, and then she and Gabe had been standing in the warm sunshine outside Angola, holding hands as the warden led Jimmy toward them and the media crowded in, shouting questions and flashing cameras.

Gabe had ordered them all back as she'd stepped toward her big brother, now so much thinner than before, with the same wounded look in his eyes that she'd seen from the dogs at the shelter. She'd wanted to take them all, give them all homes. In the end, they'd chosen only three. Or rather, the three—a scrawny female yellow Lab with two equally scrawny pups, all Katrina victims—had chosen them.

Simon had gone home with Jimmy.

Now she looked at Gabe and felt the warmth in her heart tug at the corners of her mouth. "You're early." She'd wanted to have everything cleaned up before he got home.

The gleam in his eyes turned into a wicked little twinkle. "Funny…I'm thinking I'm just in time."

She realized his intent too late, not that she would have done anything to stop him. He crossed the wrinkled plastic tarps she'd used to cover the floors and stopped a few inches from her. There, he streaked his finger along her cheek, pulled it back to reveal a smear of paint. "You look good in green."

His voice was warm and thick and turned everything inside of her liquid. "It's not green," she said indignantly. "It's olive."

"Olive, then," he said, tapping his finger to her chin. "It suits you."

She wasn't sure what came over her, what made her do it, but before she could stop herself, she lifted the small roller to his face and…well, rolled. "You, too."

Before, when she'd tried so hard to hate this man, to believe him corrupt, she'd never let herself imagine a playful side to him. She'd never imagined the naughty light that could come into his eyes, or that he would join his hand to hers for control of the paint roller and slant his mouth across hers. "You sure you want to do that?"

The slow dare washed through her. "Oh, yes," she said.

"You know what they say about starting something you don't want someone else to finish," he warned.

"Who said I don't want you to finish it?"

And then he was there, pulling her into his arms as they both surrendered the paint roller. His mouth came next, taking hers with a hunger that heated her blood. She urged him backward, toward the one part of the room she'd not covered with plastic—the big new mattress in the center. The headboard was still on order.

But then, they didn't need it for what she had in mind. And as she dragged him down with her, she shot out her foot and pulled the lamp cord from the wall, killing the light.

Because those courthouse rumors were most definitely true.

Gabriel Fontenot was at his absolute best…in the dark.

* * * * *

Watch for the last book in the MIDNIGHT SECRETS
miniseries SINS OF THE STORM
by Jenna Mills
Available September 2007 from
Silhouette Romantic Suspense.

THE ROYAL HOUSE OF NIROLI
Always passionate, always proud.

The richest royal family in the world—united
by blood and passion, torn apart by deceit and desire.

Nestled in the azure blue of the Mediterranean Sea, the majestic island of Niroli has prospered for centuries. The Fierezza men have worn the crown with passion and pride since ancient times. But now, as the king's health declines and his two sons have been tragically killed, the crown is in jeopardy.

The clock is ticking—a new heir must be found before the king is forced to abdicate. By royal decree the internationally scattered members of the Fierezza family are summoned to claim their destiny. But any person who takes the throne must do so according to The Rules of the Royal House of Niroli. Soon secrets and rivalries emerge as the descendents of this ancient royal line vie for position and power. Only a true Fierezza can become ruler—a person dedicated to their country, their people…and their eternal love!

Each month starting in July 2007,
Harlequin Presents is delighted to bring you
an exciting installment from
THE ROYAL HOUSE OF NIROLI,
in which you can follow the epic search
for the true Nirolian king.
Eight heirs, eight romances, eight fantastic stories!

Here's your chance to enjoy a sneak preview of the first book delivered to you by royal decree….

FIVE minutes later she was standing immobile in front of the study's window, her original purpose of coming in forgotten, as she stared in shocked horror at the envelope she was holding. Waves of heat followed by an icy chill surged through her body. She could hardly see the address now through her blurred vision, but the crest on its left-hand front corner stood out, its *royal* crest, followed by the address: *HRH Prince Marco of Niroli*....

She didn't hear Marco's key in the apartment door, she didn't even hear him calling out her name. Her shock was so great that nothing could penetrate it. It encased her in a kind of bubble, which only concentrated the torment of what she was suffering and branded it on her brain so that it could never be forgotten. It was only finally pierced by the sudden opening of the study door as Marco walked in.

"Welcome home, *Your Highness*. I suppose I ought

to curtsy." She waited, praying that he would laugh and tell her that she had got it all wrong, that the envelope she was holding, addressing him as Prince Marco of Niroli, was some silly mistake. But, like a tiny candle flame shivering vulnerably in the dark, her hope trembled fearfully. And then the look in Marco's eyes extinguished it as cruelly as a hand placed callously over a dying person's face to stem their last breath.

"Give that to me," he demanded, taking the envelope from her.

"It's too late, Marco," Emily told him brokenly. "I know the truth now…" She dug her teeth in her lower lip to try to force back her own pain.

"You had no right to go through my desk," Marco shot back at her furiously, full of loathing at being caught off guard and forced into a position in which he was in the wrong, making him determined to find something he could accuse Emily of. "I trusted you…."

Emily could hardly believe what she was hearing. "No, you didn't trust me, Marco, and you didn't trust me because you knew that I couldn't trust you. And you knew that because you're a liar, and liars don't trust people because they know that they themselves cannot be trusted." She not only felt sick, she also felt as though she could hardly breathe. "You are Prince Marco of Niroli… How could you not tell me who you are and still live with me as intimately as we have lived together?" she demanded brokenly.

"Stop being so ridiculously dramatic," Marco demanded fiercely. "You are making too much of the situation."

"*Too much?*" Emily almost screamed the words at him. "When were you going to tell me, Marco? Perhaps you just planned to walk away without telling me anything? After all, what do my feelings matter to you?"

"Of course they matter." Marco stopped her sharply. "And it was in part to protect them, and you, that I decided not to inform you when my grandfather first announced that he intended to step down from the throne and hand it on to me."

"To protect me?" Emily nearly choked on her fury. "Hand on the throne? No wonder you told me when you first took me to bed that all you wanted was sex. You *knew* that was the only kind of relationship there could ever be between us! You *knew* that one day you would be Niroli's king. No doubt you are expected to marry a princess. Is she picked out for you already, your *royal* bride?"

* * * * *

Look for THE FUTURE KING'S PREGNANT
MISTRESS
by Penny Jordan in July 2007,
from Harlequin Presents,
available wherever books are sold.

HARLEQUIN®

Mediterranean NIGHTS™

Experience the glamour and elegance of cruising the high seas with a new 12-book series....

MEDITERRANEAN NIGHTS

Coming in July 2007...

SCENT OF A WOMAN

by

Joanne Rock

When Danielle Chevalier is invited to an exclusive conference aboard *Alexandra's Dream,* she knows it will mean good things for her struggling fragrance company. But her dreams get a setback when she meets Adam Burns, a representative from a large American conglomerate.

Danielle is charmed by the brusque American— until she finds out he means to compete with her bid for the opportunity that will save her family business!

www.eHarlequin.com

HM38961

nocturne™

**DON'T MISS THE RIVETING CONCLUSION
TO THE RAINTREE TRILOGY**

RAINTREE: SANCTUARY

by *New York Times* bestselling author

BEVERLY
BARTON

Mercy, guardian of the Raintree
homeplace, takes a stand against
the Ansara wizards to battle for
the Clan's future.

*On sale July,
wherever books are sold.*

REQUEST YOUR FREE BOOKS!

2 FREE NOVELS PLUS 2 FREE GIFTS!

Silhouette® Romantic

SUSPENSE

Sparked by Danger, Fueled by Passion!

YES! Please send me 2 FREE Silhouette® Romantic Suspense novels and my 2 FREE gifts. After receiving them, if I don't wish to receive any more books, I can return the shipping statement marked "cancel." If I don't cancel, I will receive 4 brand-new novels every month and be billed just $4.24 per book in the U.S., or $4.99 per book in Canada, plus 25¢ shipping and handling per book plus applicable taxes, if any*. That's a savings of at least 15% off the cover price! I understand that accepting the 2 free books and gifts places me under no obligation to buy anything. I can always return a shipment and cancel at any time. Even if I never buy another book from Silhouette, the two free books and gifts are mine to keep forever.

240 SDN EEX6   340 SDN EEYJ

Name	(PLEASE PRINT)	
Address		Apt. #
City	State/Prov.	Zip/Postal Code

Signature (if under 18, a parent or guardian must sign)

Mail to the Silhouette Reader Service™:
IN U.S.A.: P.O. Box 1867, Buffalo, NY 14240-1867
IN CANADA: P.O. Box 609, Fort Erie, Ontario L2A 5X3

Not valid to current Silhouette Intimate Moments subscribers.

Want to try two free books from another line?
Call 1-800-873-8635 or visit www.morefreebooks.com.

* Terms and prices subject to change without notice. NY residents add applicable sales tax. Canadian residents will be charged applicable provincial taxes and GST. This offer is limited to one order per household. All orders subject to approval. Credit or debit balances in a customer's account(s) may be offset by any other outstanding balance owed by or to the customer. Please allow 4 to 6 weeks for delivery.

Your Privacy: Silhouette is committed to protecting your privacy. Our Privacy Policy is available online at www.eHarlequin.com or upon request from the Reader Service. From time to time we make our lists of customers available to reputable firms who may have a product or service of interest to you. If you would prefer we not share your name and address, please check here. ☐

SRS07

THE GARRISONS
A brand-new family saga begins with

THE CEO'S SCANDALOUS AFFAIR
BY ROXANNE ST. CLAIRE

Eldest son Parker Garrison is preoccupied running
his Miami hotel empire and dealing with his recently
deceased father's secret second family. Since he has
little time to date, taking his superefficient assistant
to a charity event should have been a simple plan.
Until passion takes them beyond business.

Don't miss any of the six exciting titles in
THE GARRISONS continuity, beginning in July.
Only from Silhouette Desire.

THE CEO'S SCANDALOUS AFFAIR
#1807

Available July 2007.

Silhouette®
Romantic
SUSPENSE

COMING NEXT MONTH

#1471 ONE STORMY NIGHT—Marilyn Pappano
Jennifer Randall poses as her twin to bring down her brother-in-law whom she believes brutally attacked her sister. Little does she know that the next-door neighbor she's falling for is investigating the same man.

#1472 MY SPY—Marie Ferrarella
Mission: Impassioned
When the prime minister of England discovers his daughter has been kidnapped, he turns to the one man who can return her safely. Joshua Lazlo has rescued plenty of damsels in distress, but none has compared to his latest assignment. She's more than a handful for him and the kidnappers, but there's something about his feisty target he can't resist.

#1473 FORTUNE HUNTER'S HERO—Linda Turner
Broken Arrow Ranch
He must stay at his newly inherited ranch or ownership reverts to a secret heir. She claims a Spanish mine is located on the property. Together they set out to solve the puzzle and fight an attraction that threatens more than their hearts.

#1474 SECRETS RISING—Suzanne McMinn
Haven
In the wake of a personal tragedy, Detective Jake Mallory comes to the small town of Haven to find some peace and quiet. Instead, he finds himself caught up in a series of bizarre events that all circle around a beautiful woman. But the more he investigates, the more questions arise. And the biggest question has yet to be answered…what, or who, is buried in Keely Schiffer's backyard?

SRSCNM0607